THE TWO-PLATE SOLUTION

A NOVEL OF CULINARY MAYHEM
IN THE MIDDLE EAST

Jeff Oliver

**bancroft
press**

Interior design: Tracy Copes
Cover concept: J.L. Herchenroeder
Cover: Liz Blazer
Author Photo: Stuart Tyson

HC: 978-1-61088-223-1
PB: 978-1-61088-218-7
Kindle/Mobi: 978-1-61088-225-5
Ebook: 978-1-61088-226-2
Audio: 978-1-61088-227-9

Published by Bancroft Press "Books that Enlighten"
410-358-0658
P.O. Box 65360, Baltimore, MD 21209 410-764-1967 (fax)
www.bancroftpress.com

Printed in the United States of America

To the storytellers working in reality TV

CHAPTER 1

From the very first day of production, Sara Sinek knew it was going to be a shit show. Who shoots a reality TV cooking competition in Israel while under imminent threat of a terrorist attack?

And yet, a mere fifty-six miles from a suspected ISIS base in Egypt, cameras were up on *Natural Dish-aster* season five. The network had already printed swag for what they lovingly branded *The Chosen Season™*.

At the site of the shoot, on what was a regular summer day in Eilat, Israel, the sounds of Skrillex thumped from a Vegas-like hotel. Israelis in speedos sipped cocktails under sun umbrellas. Amidst the sweet stink of sunscreen and shawarma, all luxuriated in a dazzling view of the Red Sea's emerald waters and endless coral reef.

There was, of course, the ever-present reminder of existential threat. Armed Israeli soldiers walked the perimeter and military jets streaked the distant sky. But this was Eilat; a place to forget all that, to unwind from the holy and to be content with the profane—even laugh a little. And that's exactly what everyone seemed to be doing so effortlessly.

Everyone but Sara. She sat in a production tent down the beach at the Grand Sheba Excelsior. The newly-constructed five-star resort was still receiving finishing touches before its official open. At the main gate, an electrical crew tinkered with the security system and argued loudly in Hebrew. Inside, an American reality TV production was in full swing: Production Assistants (PAs), camera-operators (ops), and producers of all kinds scurried about. At the pool, a crane extended fifty feet in the air, holding up a large platform on which a cooking station, two burners, and a small pantry had been placed.

Nine hot young American *chef-testants* were lounging around the pool. Some chefs smoked cigarettes, comparing tattoos. One chef, Tanya, wept loudly as two female chefs tried to console her. Camera and audio covered the spectacle.

"He's gone!" Tanya wept. "I miss him so much. My Brandon. His abs alone . . . so fucking hot!" As Tanya keened like a widow at a funeral, she noticed the crew quickly losing interest. Abruptly ceasing her crying, she asked: "You guys need me to do a safety?"

In the control room tent, Sara Sinek watched the situation wearily on a quad of TV monitors. She pulled off her *Misfits* baseball cap and let her long black hair fall over her face like the creepy girl in *The Ring*. Then she stood up, all 5'11" of her, and shook herself out, Kundalini-Yoga-style, before falling back into her chair.

"You okay?" a story coordinator seated behind her asked.

"Just cringing again," said Sara, putting her cap back into place. "For once, I'd like to experience a warm flush of pride; even the pleasant tingle of intellectual stimulation… Nope. I get full-body cringes from Chef Tanya's theatrics."

As interim Showrunner, Sara was sitting between Strider, the Lead Director (so nicknamed because he supposedly took everything in stride) and Zack, the Director of Photography (DP). Sara wore the standard half ninja/half skater-boy crew outfit—black-on-black cotton with Chuck Taylors.

"Want me to keep covering this abomination?" Strider asked her.

"Is a pig's pussy pork?" Sara replied.

"Holy shit! Can I marry that phrase?" asked Zack.

"Let me put it another way," said Sara. "Only if you want to work on season six. Yes, please continue to cover Tanya's emotional breakdown."

"Another season of blowing The Network? Sounds like a blast," said Strider.

"And if the blowing's decent, they take credit for that too," added Zack.

Sara gave the DP a fist bump for that one, adding, "Ugh, BJs... I think I gave half of one in high school before swearing it off for life. If anyone sees Colin Mechlowitz, tell him I apologize for the braces, and that his boner definitely turned me gay."

"Boss Lady wants the Tanya safety," Strider said into a microphone.

"Close on the tears," Sara added.

"And get close on those crocodile tears, please," parroted Strider.

Sara stood up and headed for the exit. She passed her boss, Warren Lopez, who snoozed on an army cot with a bag of pita chips on his belly.

"Listen up, people," Sara said into her walkie. "Unless you're C-Camera, time to reset for the next climb. Once that's done, feel free to go back to sleep."

The crew leapt into action. Culinary sprinted to replenish ingredients and replace dirty pots and pans; audio swapped mics; the art department touched up a smudged logo; and producers buzzed around the pool texting story notes on their iPhones back to Post in Burbank.

Sara stepped into the sunlight and lit a cigarette. She tried to focus on the natural beauty before her but was distracted. She didn't like how loose resort security was: one of the *Krav-MaGuards* she'd hired was napping in a Jeep while the other was lounging about in the shade, swiping his fingers over an iPad like he was scratching lotto tickets. Sara pulled out her phone and scrolled through the newest Terrorist Threat Alert: "ISIS movement confirmed near the border. Threat level upped to medium-high."

"*So fucked,*" Sara whispered to herself, then drew heavily on her cigarette.

"You the *metumtam* [Hebrew for "moron"] in charge here?" asked a female medic with an Israeli accent.

"Second idiot, actually," Sara said. "Unless you want to wake the circus bear in the tent."

"Ah, so you speak Hebrew? Big whoop. You're freakishly tall. You know this?"

"*Bevakasha* [Hebrew for "thank you"]."

The Medic shoved some papers into Sara's hand. "The moron you almost just killed? These release him into hospital care. Sign twice and initial there."

"How is he?" Sara asked.

"Concussion. Twenty stitches, easy."

"When do you think he'll be able to . . . "

"Cook?" the Medic scoffed. "This is *Breaking Bad*?"

"We considered calling the show *Baking Bad* but cakes aren't rating."

"Oh, so you're someone funny," the Medic said.

"Why not?" said Sara.

The Medic rolled her eyes. "Whether he can cook depends on the scans. He'll need a couple of days rest at least, much more if there's bleeding inside his skull. Can't you find another crash test dummy to replace him, or have you killed off the alternates?"

The Medic brashly lifted a cigarette from Sara's pack and lit up, giving Sara the chance to look the Medic over. She had bright green eyes, olive skin, and a mess of lush black curls—a real beauty under all that righteous indignation. Sara noticed a burn scar along the side of her neck shaped like a panther, which the Medic instinctively covered with her wrist as she smoked.

The "crash test dummy" the Medic was referring to—actually a two-time James Beard Award-winning chef—had been carted away in an ambulance only minutes before. He was daily carnage from that morning's *Jugular Challenge,* a mainstay in the *Natural Dish-aster* format.

"Prepare to reach culinary heights you never thought possible," the host, Chef CJ Bazemore, had said to the ten hot young chefs lined up next to the pool. Bazemore, who'd gained notoriety on Facebook Live for deboning a pig in under a minute, had earned an audition for the hosting role based on his robust social media following. That, along with his boyish good looks, bright blue eyes, and the ability to arch his eyebrows like Jack Black had sealed the deal. Bazemore's only sticking point, other than an exorbitant wardrobe budget, mostly for chef jackets made entirely of silk, was that he insisted on writing his own copy.

"Each of you will climb that crazy-ass fifty-foot crane, step onto the platform, and cook a bible-themed *amuse bouche* with only the ingredients you find under the cloche, plus a limited pantry." The chefs looked up at the crane, which extended over the pool, and gave the cameras the astonished looks that would assure them more screen time. "But as always on *Natural Dish-aster,* there's a twist," said Bazemore, arching an eyebrow in that evilicious way that made him a perennial Snapchat celebrity. "You will be cooking over a trap door, and when your ten minutes are up, that trap door will fall, you with it, fifty feet into the unforgiving water."

CHEF BRANDON (REALITY-STYLE INTERVIEW): "I've had vertigo since my foster mother died in a hang gliding accident when I was eight years old. Plus, I can't swim. Okay, laugh. Guess who's the black guy who can't swim this season? I don't think I can handle this challenge... let alone... [frankenbite edit] create... a bible-themed *amuse bouche*... in ten minutes."

"Question," said Chef Joaquim. "Can we cook a New Testament amuse bouche, or does this shit have to be racist?"

"Up to you," replied an off-camera producer. "Just be prepared to explain its historical relevance to the judges."

Bazemore continued: "As always, a heckler from the opposing team will be assigned to each of you and will borrow my megaphone to ensure they're heard. So who's first? Let's see... Chef Brandon from team Mise En Place?"

Brandon lowered his head like a man condemned to the gallows. His forehead glazed with sweat and his fingertips tingled. But as he climbed the ladder to the platform, what triggered Brandon's anxiety was less his emotionally wrenching backstory, or even his inability to survive once he hit the water, but more that he knew right away who his heckler would be: Tanya.

The mousy blonde in daisy dukes and purple eye-shadow had trained in Japan with Michikutu, where she'd gained not just a competence in the *chirashizushi* technique, but also a mastery of ninja mind games, which she used mercilessly, and to great effect, against her competitors on all the cable cooking competitions. She had won three straight on *Chef, Marry, Kill.*

Chef Brandon had made the mistake of accepting Tanya's challenge of a Café Patrón drink-off the night before, and a hazy cringe-fest was now playing in his mind: the two of them atop the washing machine; she performing reverse cowgirl on the laundry room floor; and then...

"Why do you cry when you come, Brandon?" Tanya's voice, both nasal and raspy, boomed over the megaphone. "When we did it in the laundry room last night, you wept like I stole your binky. Why?"

Brandon shook off a full-body cringe as the rest of the cast members laughed. He reached the platform and pulled open the silver cloche: a bag of fresh pita, a whole swordfish, and four plump Israeli figs.

CHEF BRANDON (INT.): "When I saw the figs and the swordfish, I knew right away I would do a crudo with miso foam on a toasted pita brioche drizzled with fig compote. It's a tricky dish since you have to micro-fillet the swordfish... plus... (frankenbite*) I'm going to plunge to my death at any moment."

Brandon stuck to the basics he'd learned during his externship at *South 44* in Miami and then as Sous Chef to Heston Blumenthal at *Fat Duck* in Berkshire. He readied the liquid nitrogen.

CHEF JOAQUIM (INT.): "Of course Brandon goes molecular gastronomy. Can that pretentious *pendejo* even make toast without it exploding in a cloud of smoke?"

"Why do you cry when you come, Brandon?" Tanya yelled. "You had snot running down your face!"

Four minutes in, Brandon's figs had caramelized ever so tenderly. Honey and lemon played gently on paper-thin slices of swordfish. And as he sautéed, chiffoned, glazed, garnished, and eventually plated, Brandon used near-Ghandian discipline to block out Tanya and her yelling about a *"teary-eyed orgasm!"* It was a masterpiece; a sumptuous morsel of emulsified genius. But once plated, a full forty seconds remained on the clock, and that extra time proved to be a killer.

With nothing to do but think about the trap door and the water below, a muscular boa of anxiety slithered around Brandon's neck and tightened. All his fears rushed to the surface— his vertigo, fear of sharks, drowning. Brandon's face broke out in tingly sweat and his vasovagal vein clenched as images of his foster mother plummeting to her death beamed on the IMAX screen in his skull and Tanya's voice echoed slow and Vader-like: *"Yoooour whoooole face waaaas coooovered in teeeeeeeears!"*

The segment producers had accounted for many possibilities: chefs who might step off the trap door at the last second; chefs with knives still in their hands when they fell; even the possibility of a chef getting caught on the door. But none had expected someone to faint before the trap door even opened. But that's exactly what happened. In Brandon's body, blood went every-which-way except to his brain. His eyes rolled to the back of his head and he buckled to his knees, slapping his beautiful dish off the cooking station and causing it to fly off the platform and into the pool fifty feet below.

"You dropped your damn plate, jackass!" yelled Tanya.

When the ominous click of the trap door triggered and the metal grate fell, pure instinct made Brandon cling by his fingertips. He hung there for several seconds, giving the producers hope. *Maybe his unconscious-self would climb back up?* No such luck. Chef Brandon let go, awkwardly falling backwards but then splaying out into a mid-air cartwheel that seemed so graceful that hope sprang again in the producers' hearts.

Perhaps Brandon felt a similar sense of optimism, because he awoke mid-air with a strange smile on his face, feeling pride swell within him that he could enjoy an entire quartersecond before his head clipped against his own plate of food and everything went black.

"Medics! Goddammit, get out there!"

In dashed the medics, sirens blaring. The Line Producer nervously fished out insurance forms to make sure they were covered. Tanya, in a touching display, ran into the water to be at her lover's side as he was strapped to a gurney and carted off. Blood poured down Brandon's face and neck from a gash on the side of his head.

But just as the medics lifted him onto the ambulance, he came to. Brandon slowly raised his fist and whispered: "Go Team Mise En Place," to which his four teammates responded in roars like it was the *Braveheart* speech, and didn't stop until the ambulance drove off.

"Aw crap, now they're fired up," Tanya said to the camera.

Out from the production tent, Strider strode, donning a pair of white-framed Ray-Bans and calling out to repo camera for Tanya's climb. Tanya bounded up the plank, cooked a simple swordfish sashimi drizzled with date syrup, took a deep hypnotic breath, and before the other team could even heckle her that she'd murdered Chef Brandon with talk of his own orgasm, the trap door gave and she sailed gracefully down into the water below. A completed dish, and thus a win regardless of quality. Team Amuse Bouche: One. Team Mise En Place: Zero.

"It was the single stupidest stunt I've ever seen, and I did three years in the Israeli military," the Medic was saying to Sara. She blew smoke in Sara's general direction to punctuate her disdain. "Do these chefs even realize they've put their lives in the hands of a *maniac?* Can this show make you that rich? "

"Last year's winner signed an overall with Bourdain's company."

"So that is at least something."

"Make you a deal," Sara said, sensing an opening. "I'll keep an extra eye out on safety for you—no more shenanigans at all. In return, you'll instruct those security guards by the gate to quit napping on the job. They won't listen to a thing I say. Honestly, I don't even know if they understand English."

"So tell them in Hebrew," the Medic said. "Anyway, you don't have the authority to make such a deal."

"I do," said Sara. "But even more important, you have my word. From now on, nothing dangerous on set. I promise you."

The Medic saw the sincerity in Sara's eyes and almost conceded when a breathless Associate Producer ran up to them. "Bazemore is refusing to get in the tiger cage. Says it's not in his contract."

Sara pressed her temples. "Ask if he'll do a bear."

"Copy that," said the AP and ran off.

"Wow, an American with chutzpah," the Medic scoffed, stubbing out her cigarette. "Is it exhausting to be such a total cliché?"

Sara didn't have a chance to answer that rhetorical question before total chaos broke out on set. It started with a shriek from Tanya, followed by the sound of gunshots spraying the air.

It all happened in seconds. Along the road, three army Jeeps sped wildly towards the set and screeched to a halt. Then a dozen men in army khakis, black ski masks, and red kafyias burst out holding semi-automatics in the air. *Where was security? Suddenly gone.* Sara stepped in front of the Medic, landing a protective hand on her arm. The Medic, a tough Israeli chick, shrugged it off.

"Who's in charge here?" the tallest terrorist barked in thickly accented English. "Stand before me, Infidel!"

Warren Lopez, the hard-partying, barely-working Executive Producer and owner of It-Is-What-It-Is Productions (IIWIIP), woke from his nap, brushed pita chips off his belly, and uncharacteristically declared his role as leader. "Uh, yeah. That's me. What can I do you gentlemen for?"

Two masked men ran up to Lopez and jabbed him in the ribs with a gun butt. Almost the very second Lopez buckled to his knees, they threw a black hood over his head.

"Who's next?" asked the tall terrorist.

Sara took a step forward, but this time it was the Medic who pulled the back of her shirt, stopping Sara in her tracks.

"Wait a second. Just wait one fucking second," Chef Tanya jumped in. "That's the ambulance driver. He's got Brandon's blood on his shoe. Look! This is bullshit. These guys aren't terrorists. They're phonies!"

Tanya pointed at them. The terrorists had no response. They shuffled and looked around aimlessly.

The leader finally puffed up. "Yes, we are terrorists. We're bad men from ISIS," he said.

"Yeah, and I'm Daniel Boulud," said Tanya.

Lopez lifted his hood and called out to Strider, "Stay rolling. We'll fix it in post. Tanya, would you just suspend disbelief for a minute? We're trying to set up your next challenge."

CJ Bazemore strutted out with freshly written copy in hand: "Teams, get ready for the next twist. You are no longer battling each other. These crazy Islamic terrorists are now your culinary foes, and it's up to you to banish them from the land of milk and honey using only your chef knives." There was an awkward pause, after which Bazemore asked Strider if he needed him to do a safety.

Lopez sighed. "Hey, terrorists? That's your cue. Jesus Christ!"

The tall terrorist coughed. "Oh, uh. Long live ISIS! Down with Israel and America! See you at dawn for your Cannibal Challenge."

The terrorists all shot blanks into the air and drove off in their Jeeps like a bunch of clowns. On cue, the chefs started booing and saying dumb shit like, "We're going to terrorize *you*, motherfuckers!"

"And that's lunch," the Second AD called out. The crew dropped everything and sprinted to the meal tent.

Lopez tossed his hood to a PA and walked up to Sara, who was still standing next to the Medic. "Network called last night, pissed," he said. "They have a new mandate. All about higher stakes—real stuff too. They're getting killed by *Run Around Sous*, so they forced my hand. Make the Challenge about ISIS terrorists. Told me I couldn't tell a soul so that it's shot crazy-style. It was all their idea."

"What about the schedule?" asked Sara.

"Screw the schedule. They approved an overage," Lopez said. "American culinary heroes versus Islamic terrorists. Writes itself." Lopez grabbed for his vibrating cell phone. "Aw, fuck, it's my wife. Hold… Hi, honey. No, just working. Well, sometimes I have to put it on silent. Well, I'm sorry if I'm missing the baby's bubble bath. Can you snapchat it to me?"

Sara's headache intensified as Lopez walked off.

"This is madness," the Medic said, storming off. "How do you sleep?"

"What about our deal?" said Sara. "You promised to talk to the guards in exchange for…"

CHAPTER 2

Despite what all of them expected to be a logistical night-mare the following day, a night of compulsory hard partying was already underway for the crew. Just about everyone had headed to The Golden Buddha, a newly opened Thai-themed dance bar just down-beach. The paint was not yet dry on the walls, and port-o-potties in the alley were functioning as the only restrooms, but the bar offered "ten-shekel shots" (less than $3 U.S.), and there was enough sexual curiosity between the Israeli locals and American crew to guarantee a wild evening.

Sara hung back in her room and dialed up her brother Nathan on Facetime, as she did every night at what was mid-morning in Reno, Nevada. But when the call picked up, instead of Nathan answering, a thirty-something Indian man stared impatiently back through the screen.

"I'm done, Sara," the man said. "Your mom hasn't paid me in two months. I get here, she's gone. I can't do this anymore. I quit."

"You say that every time I call, Simon," said Sara. "Where's Nathan?"

"Playing Minecraft."

"I thought we agreed to limit that."

"I'm not limiting anything, Sara. I'm done—walking out. I

can't pay my rent."

"I sent money two weeks ago," said Sara.

"Never saw it, but that explains your mom's recent casino binge. Goodbye."

"Look at me. I'll immediately wire money directly into your account. It'll be available to you in three days. How much total does she owe you?"

"Including what she borrowed? Forty-five hundred."

"I'll take care of it. Nathan's fourth on the waiting list at Newberry Academy. Should only be a few more weeks until we hear…"

"You think you're going to afford that fancy place?" Simon scoffed. "They do credit checks, Sara. By the way, a couple of shady dudes keep dropping by asking for your mother. Big dudes with neck tattoos. Seems like I'm not the only one she owes."

"I'll handle that."

"I'll work to the end of the week, but that's it. I'm sorry, Sara. I have a Masters in autism research. I'm not a baby sitter."

"Put Nathan on."

Nathan appeared on-screen. He looked like Sara, but fifteen years younger and without all the hard edges. He wore a loosefitting pajama shirt, and his boyish Jewfro was pressed to one side, bed-head fashion. Nathan looked off-screen with a mischievous grin that Sara recognized well.

"Minecraft? Really?" she said.

"Mom said it was okay," said Nathan.

"Mom's not in charge. That's why I call every day."

"Is forty-five hundred dollars enough to buy our video-game theatre?" Nathan asked.

"It's a start."

"Zane says it will cost way more."

"Who's Zane?"

"Zane says it's not the theatre that costs a lot, it's the licensing fees. Zane says the only way to make money in theatres is popcorn. Zane said that even super-old games like *Zelda* are going to cost a lot of money, and there's no way we're ever going to open the theatre unless we win the lottery. Do you buy lottery tickets?"

"Who's Zane?"

"One of the guys looking for Mom," Nathan said. "He has a tattoo on his neck. I think it's a bull, but the horns are on fire. Says he has something for her but wants to give it directly to her. They keep missing each other, like the most epic game of tag ever."

"Nathan, listen to me. Do not talk to that guy."

"But he comes all the time . . . and Mom's always out, even one time when I was sure she was home. Then, last time, Zane brought another, even bigger guy. Simon says he's a famous UFC fighter or something. He's got tattoos of broken bones on his hands."

"Nathan, where's Mom?"

"Probably out getting what the guys want." Nathan shrugged. "Hey, *Combat Rush* will probably be expensive to license too, right? It's underrated and word's getting out. What about *Brainpop*? Although it's more of an educational app, it's still sort of a game, right?"

"Management will have to discuss," said Sara. "Nathan, who do you call if there's an emergency?"

"911."

"What's our emergency phrase?"

"Will you sing it if I tell you?"

"No."

"Then I don't know."

"Fine, I'll sing."

"*Chasing Pavement* is the worst song ever written," Nathan said, reluctantly.

"Good. Tell Mom to call me as soon as she gets in."

"Cueing music."

And then... Adele, *Chasing Pavement.* Nathan grabbed a comb, Sara a walkie battery, and the siblings sang the pop-hit karaoke-style all the way through before hanging up. It was their daily ritual.

The Golden Buddha Bar was turning into a schvitz lodge. A flashing neon dance floor of spastic Israeli resort workers and drunken crew grinded to Major Lazer. What united Americans and Israelis most was their adoration of mindless pop combined with their ability to make fun of it at the same time. The Israelis were more into it, closing their eyes and hooting wildly, but the crew matched their laughter, and when a Ke$ha remix blasted on, they knew it by heart.

At the bar were some off-duty army guys, and Sara noticed the Medic amongst them. One of the drunker guys was pushing a drink on her. She barked a refusal at him and he put up his hands in submission.

Lopez intercepted Sara on his way to the can. "How's my rockstar Co-EP? Crack the story yet?" he said.

"Like you said, ISIS terrorists versus American culinary heroes," said Sara. "Writes itself. Double eliminations. We'll need the terrorists to move into the cast house."

"You think?" Lopez said.

"Separate wings, but we need the drama," said Sara. "And the hook-ups."

"Hook-ups with ISIS. Not too polarizing?"

"Forbidden fruit, yes, but also shocking to liberal viewers

who'll have to face their feelings about sleeping with the enemy. Not to mention some interesting digital extras."

"I like the way you think."

"Casting did a solid job; half these guys graduated Cordon Bleu. We should have a good match. We'll just have to fudge the end to make sure the good guys win."

"*L'chaim* to that," Lopez said. "Oh, forgot to tell you: Strider's out in the Bedouin desert for the next few days shooting a development piece for me. Bedouin camel warriors are still a thing, believe it or not. Nomad Network's paying for the sizzle."

"But…"

"Oh, don't stress. I've seen you direct. You're a natural. Besides, you'll have Zack."

"I'll have Zack," Sara sighed.

Lopez took a long swig of his orange blossom vodka tonic. "You ever been married, Sinek? Didn't think so. See, the thing about marriage is you're a team for a while, and you think, 'How can anyone compete with a team?' You're chasing your dreams, got someone to laugh at all the bullshit with, sex is all the time. Then, one day, *SNAP*, you're a prisoner to a bank account and there's a stranger in your bed glaring at you every time you play Sugar Rush on your Blackberry." Lopez shook his head slowly and set his glass down on the bar. "Hey, barkeep?" he said. "Give my rockstar showrunner here what the locals drink. I gotta piss."

Lopez threw a wad of shekels on the bar and walked off.

"Bedouin camel warriors," Sara muttered.

The bartender, a pink-mohawked nymph in a mid-riff shirt, handed Sara a wine glass topped with an umbrella that smelled like petrol and rosewater. She winked before walking away, maybe letting Sara know that the door was open to flirt, or maybe she was just playing for a bigger tip. Sara looked along the bar and caught eyes with the Medic. She frowned at the sight of her, so Sara frowned back theatrically, managing to earn a grin.

Just then, the drunken army guy shoved another drink in the Medic's face, spilling a good half of it on her. She slapped him away, and again his hands went in the air. "Okay, okay, woman!" he said.

Sara pulled out her cell phone and texted her mother: "Leave the casino or I call social services."

She looked up at a TV screen across from the bar. Some new terrorist group named Mal-Malaika was on the news. A bombing in Haifa, Israel. Seven dead. IDF raid of Mal-Malaika headquarters. Shootout but no bodies. Perpetrators on the run. *Should end badly*, Sara thought. The dance floor erupted when Nicki Minaj came on.

A text buzzed back from Sara's mother: "Almost home! Car broke down—something about combustion. $2,000! Wire $$ plz?" Sara sighed and tucked the phone back in her jeans.

Over at the bar, the drunken army guy was getting handsy with the Medic. His buddies laughed as he grinded up to her holding two shot glasses high in the air. "Come on, baby, you're hanging around too many idiot Americans. Let's have some fun." When he leaned in for a kiss, the Medic pushed him away and one shot glass went flying. He grabbed her arm. "Why you have to act like such a hard-ass bitch?"

Sara took a swig of her rosewater petrol and headed over. She decided to go old-school.

"Hey," Sara said to the drunken soldier.

The soldier couldn't believe his eyes. He dropped the Medic's arm. "Who is this *fuckim?*" He turned to his friends and laughed. He then swiveled and put a hand on Sara's shoulder. His thick, drunken breath invaded her nostrils. "My giant lesbian friend," the soldier slurred. "Do you know what *titsim godolim* are? It's how you say in idiot land, big titties? This one has *titsim godolim* for miles."

Sara said nothing, looked at the hand on her shoulder, and then at the other guys. *He didn't look so big, but trained. It will take precision timing.*

"What's wrong? You don't speak?" the soldier said. "Are you retard? Are you a retarded Mrs. Trump? Do you hear me in there?"

Sara caught the gaze of the Medic, who gave her a "he's-not-*your*-problem" look, but Sara couldn't help herself. "That word you just used," she said. "We don't use it anymore in the States. It's outdated, low class. Offensive too. So unless you want trouble, I suggest you—"

The Medic chose that moment to forcibly drop a barstool onto the soldier's nose, with the blood spraying Sara's face. In less than a second, the Medic was grabbing the guy by the hair and giving him a quick kick with her knee. From behind, one of the guy's friends made a move to grab the Medic.

Sara chopped the guy in the neck, grabbed him by his ear, and looked hard into his eyes. The guy put his hand out in submission and fell to his knees gasping for breath. The other guy backed off like it was all none of his business.

"Grab some air?" the Medic said.

"Lead the way," said Sara.

They walked out of the bar into the cool night breeze. Sara lit a cigarette and the Medic grabbed it from her mouth.

"Don't you ever buy your own?" Sara asked.

"Name's Ruti," the Medic said. "And you are Sara Sinek, Co-Executive Producer of this freak show. Nice IMDB page—*Cook's Kingdom, Mega Chef*—and suddenly you're in charge. Quick rise for a *metumtam.*"

"You Googled me."

"Of course. But I learned much more about you just now." Ruti blew a perfect smoke ring. "How long did you serve in IDF?"

"I don't follow."

Ruti scoffed. "Look, I recognize that chop you did on the soldier's neck and your pulling of his ear. You didn't learn that at Jewish summer camp."

"Krav Maga. It's all the rage in West Hollywood," said Sara.

"Okay, I get it. You're Ms. Showbiz now," Ruti said. "But I know Israeli military training when I see it. And you know what else I know? You're a terrible singer. Worst Adele cover I ever heard."

"You're full-on spying on me."

"You pissed me off today. I needed something on you, and I got it." She lifted her cell phone and played a video of Sara singing Adele, which the Medic had shot through the window of her hotel room. "Your brother, he's..."

"He's my brother," Sara said, a hard edge in her voice. She pulled out another cigarette.

"Right," Ruti nodded. "I have a cousin. She is also... my cousin. So I delete."

They walked back to the resort grounds and into the main lobby. Janitors and cleaning staff, still prepping for the official opening, nodded reverentially at Ruti. Sara gave her a curious look.

"My father ran a hotel here years ago, before the land was bought for development," Ruti said. "He made a deal with the bosses that no matter what happens to the hotel, the staff keep their jobs. Even though he is dead now, they all still know me as the boss' daughter."

"Sounds like a good man," said Sara.

"He was. But bad men got him. So that's that."

Ruti led Sara to a staff-only door, through the laundry room, and onto the stage of the empty pavilion space where crew meetings were held each morning. There was a ladder behind a velvet curtain that led up into the rafters.

"Coming?" Ruti said, climbing up. "No staring at my ass,

metumtam."

Sara followed. At the top of the ladder was a small audio mix room that overlooked the stage. Inside was an army cot, a mini-fridge, and an iPod speaker.

"Secret love nest?" Sara asked.

"More like a hideout," said Ruti. "Matisyahu is scheduled to perform here when the hotel opens next month, so it's a big deal we have an engineering space. But no one will use this until then, so it's all mine. Plus, I get to eavesdrop on your fancy production meetings. You know you have a slight public speaking problem, right? You sometimes stammer a bit when you talk to the crew."

"I'm working on it."

"Meditation?"

"Xanax," said Sara.

"Nothing to be ashamed of," Ruti said, sitting down on the cot. "Hey, you want to play a game with me?"

"Does it involve public speaking?"

"Little bit. Rules are I ask you a question about your life and you answer to my complete satisfaction."

"Sounds like an interrogation."

"Each time I'm happy with your answer, I remove an article of clothing."

"More promising," said Sara. "What if my answer isn't up to snuff?"

"I add clothes."

Sara leaned up against the soundboard. "Shoot."

"Military training?" Ruti asked.

"U.S. Special Forces for eight years, then liaison to IDF," said Sara.

"Where did you serve?" Ruti pulled off her shirt, revealing a silky bra.

"Afghanistan. Lebanon. Gaza."

"When did you get out?"

"Seven years ago."

"Why?" Ruti flipped off her sandals.

"You don't need to know all that," said Sara.

"No problem," Ruti said. She picked up her shirt from off the floor and began pulling it back on.

"It'll change the mood."

"Let me judge," Ruti said.

"Okay, okay. Hold your roll," Sara said. She sighed. "Back when I was inducted, my mother agreed to be part of a documentary about parents with autistic kids. I think they paid her five hundred bucks, which she needed pretty badly at the time. The producers said they wanted to educate people, to do a public service. Turned out it was a reality TV freak show. My brother's condition was used as comic relief.

"One day while I was home on leave, a producer left lying around a binder with the show budget. The list of salaries blew my mind. Four grand a week for some of these clowns to stand around doing nothing. Even with military pay, I had debt. So what can I say? I switched careers for the money."

"Sounds also like you wanted a bit of revenge. You were tricked into letting your brother be exploited, so now you become the exploiter to take back the power. It's a fuck-off."

"That your professional assessment, Ms. Freud?"

"It is. But guess what? You won the game," said Ruti.

"How do you figure?"

"Well, I was just going to fool around with you before, but I'm a sucker for a good sob story," Ruti said, unsnapping her bra. "So, it's going to have to be full-on sex."

What happened next was a blur. Lights came on and there was a ton of yelling below. Ruti shot up in bed. Sara, pulling on her pants, peered down onto the performance pavilion.

"Hey, relax," said one voice from the pavilion. In a mad scramble, members of the crew were pulling on cargo shorts and covering up with bed sheets, shoved by men in black ski masks wielding machine guns. "Walk!" the gunmen barked.

"Dude, it's four in the morning," one of the camera guys complained. "I was sleeping cause call time's not 'til six. What the fuck?"

"Shut your mouth!" yelled the gunman.

Terrorists. But not the ones hired by the network. Those guys were down there, too, hands behind their heads. Everyone—PAs, tech, story, culinary producers, an ashen-looking Lopez, and a couple of resort staff on night shift—all herded from their rooms into the pavilion space and told to get down on the floor. A prank? Too rough for a prank.

Ruti grabbed her phone but there was no service. *Had they taken out the guards?* She panicked.

Sara popped a pill.

"Empty your pockets onto the floor!" the terrorists demanded. "Cell phone, iPad, Google Cardboard, everything." The crew obeyed. The armed men in masks stuffed it all into green duffle bags.

Pacing the pavilion stage was a tall, thin man with gold-rimmed glasses and a graying moustache. Dressed like a college professor—tweed jacket, khakis, button-down shirt—he tenderly held his left hand, which was covered by a large bandage speckled with blood. When the crowd settled, the man walked to the front of the stage.

"My sincerest apologies for the early wake-up, friends," he said. "I run with savages and they must be reminded to be gentle. My name is Izzeldin Al-Asari. I am the leader of Mal-Malaika, the peaceful group erroneously accused of a recent bombing in Haifa. We are currently being hunted down by Israeli police for something we did not do. We escaped their initial assassination attempt, but they are a determined bunch. So, we are here as fugitives . . . and we kindly ask your assistance and cooperation."

Al-Asari shook his head and smiled as if he couldn't believe he had just described his own predicament. "So, who's in charge here? Who is the great leader of *Natural Dish-aster: Season Five?*" There was silence as eyes cast down. "No one wants to fess up? Fine, I'll check the call sheet from the top. Warren Lopez?" Al-Asari stepped off the stage and walked right up to Lopez, who was pale as a sheet. "Ah, the fearless leader. Stand up, please."

"I don't have anything," Lopez pleaded. "We're a reality TV production. A cooking competition. We're sympathetic to your cause, believe me, and we don't want any trouble."

"Oh, I know all about it. Heroic American chefs versus evil Islamic terrorists. Sounds awfully progressive to me, and gripping television too," said Al-Asari. "Not to worry, Mr. Lopez. A helicopter will be here to pick us up in only a few days. But we'll have to lay low until then. We must be invisible. So, I ask you, as creative leader here, how are we going to do this? How can we be hidden now that we've aroused so much attention?"

Lopez thought hard, then his eyes lit up with what seemed to be his first great idea as a TV producer in years. "I got it!" he said. "We'll hide you all in the gear room. Keep your men hidden until the helicopter comes. We'll get you meals. You can shower up. We won't tell anyone. Not a soul. Right, everyone? No one makes a peep, or you're fired." Everyone nodded furiously.

"Done!" Lopez smiled. "We all want the same thing, see?"

Al-Asari eyed Lopez. "Must you be first to die?" he said.

Several crewmembers sobbed; an AP went faint. Al-Asari motioned to one of the armed terrorists, who poked Lopez with his machine gun.

Lopez whimpered, "I'll think of something else. Gimme a second..."

Then a loud commotion from outside the pavilion was heard—a female voice so shrill and nasal it made Fran Drescher sound like James Earl Jones. "Jesus Christ, boys, no need to push. I'm wearing Manolo Blahnik heels!" Everyone turned to see who belonged to that awful voice, but when the door opened, only Warren showed any sign of recognition.

The squawking human parrot who entered the pavilion flanked by real terrorists was none other than his wife, Sharon. She wore a patterned silk blouse, knee-high leather boots, and an enormous, bejeweled purse. It was as if an entire Nordstrom Rack had exploded onto her.

"I just get off of an eleven-hour flight and this is the welcome I get?" she said. "Jesus, it smells like open ass in here. Warren? Warren, get these goons off me."

When Lopez understood just what was happening, he looked up to the heavens, but not to question his wife's bad fortune—*to question his.* The idea of being assaulted by real Islamic terrorists was bad enough, but having his wife there to complain shrilly in his ear for God-only-knows-how-long was far too much to bear.

Lopez felt he had only one choice. So he grabbed for the gun. A terrorist grabbed him, a brief struggle ensued, and then the gun went off with a flash. A single bullet shot into Lopez's foot. "*Aargh!*" Lopez collapsed onto the floor as his shoe filled with blood.

"You fucking shot me! My foot... my goddamn foot!"

Panic erupted as the terrorist raised his gun to the crowd. Lopez squirmed as a PA wrapped a t-shirt around his foot to slow the bleeding. His wife ran to his side.

"Warren, why is this happening?" she said. "I haven't even taken a bath yet, and this? I stink, Warren. What about my bags? My photo album? I organized every last picture from the baptism. I can't lose it—it took me weeks to organize."

"Sharon!" Lopez wailed. "We're being held hostage by fucking terrorists and they fucking shot me! Now, will you please forget about the goddamn photo album!"

Sharon turned to Al-Asari and waved her arm, triggering a cacophony of clattering silver bracelets. "Yoo-hoo, Guy-In-Charge? I have a Dead Sea spa appointment on Tuesday that I refuse to miss. They made me pre-pay. Any ETA here?"

Al-Asari squinted, pained by the spectacle he was witnessing. "Put these two in the gear supply closet," he said, turning away. "They deserve each other."

The terrorists lifted Lopez, elevating his foot, then picked up his wife.

"No, wait," Lopez said. "Not with her in the closet. Anything but that… pleeeease!"

"Take them," instructed Al-Asari. He slapped his forehead as they left the room.

Up in the audio booth above the stage, Sara pulled on her shirt and headed for the ladder.

"What are you doing?" said Ruti, tugging at her. "Sara, come back here."

Sara climbed down the ladder slowly. She held up a free hand as all guns pointed her way. "I'm unarmed," Sara said.

"Who are you?" Al-Asari said. "Identify yourself immediately."

"Second in command, Sara Sinek." She stepped off the ladder and onto the stage. "You can check the call sheet."

"Ah, Co-Executive Producer Sinek. Welcome. Well, I hope you have a good plan for us, because if it's stupid, apparently we shoot you in the foot."

"Quick question first," said Sara.

"You get only one," Al-Asari said.

"Can any of your men cook?"

CHAPTER 3

In the new regime, the first order of business was updating social media. Crew had been complaining about bad Wi-Fi since arriving, so it wasn't a stretch for everyone to send out an off-the-grid message, but it required supervision. The English-speaking terrorists watched closely as crew updated Snapchat, Instagram, and Facebook with variations of: "Ghosting a few days. See you sluts on the flipside and save the good shit for when I phoenix. #digitaldiet #darkages #missmebitches." Still, more than a few days without a check-in would be unfathomable to the crew's family, friends, followers, and *Words with Friends* opponents without some kind of larger announcement. They'd have to figure that out when they got there.

Under the terrorists' watchful eye, Ruti shut down the hotel's Wi-Fi and phone lines except for the hardline in the main office. She called the resort staff who were, so far, unaware of the terrorist infiltration, and told them that they would be spraying the resort for termites so they could all take a fully paid three-day vacation.

The pavilion was set up as a holding area. Cots were arranged, gear gathered, and showers for crew organized alphabetically. Luckily, the cook, a robust elderly woman with big rosy cheeks, was among those previously captured, so breakfast remained a sumptuous spread of sufganyot, shakshuka with cumin, labneh cheese, and thick Turkish coffee. Once the crew got fed and caffeinated, they were back on the job, and even the biggest pot-smoking slacker in reality TV turned into a Navy Seal when they got a call sheet. In fact, it wasn't long before the crew got impatient with the terrorists. By precisely eight a.m., all crew had gathered by the docks for the *Cannibal Challenge* and it was cameras up as usual.

The only lingering issue to resolve was what to do with the fake terrorists. Ruti let Sara know that Eilat police took regular headcounts of resort action from a checkpoint tower on the beach, and that even a fluctuation of a few heads might set off red flags. Local authorities knew about the "fake terrorist" shoot, and weren't happy about it, but the presence of more than nine masked men would mean instant trouble.

The problem with hiding the fake terrorists outright (or killing them, as several real terrorists suggested) is that someone needed to cook during the challenges. Culinary competence could be faked with sharp cutaways and editing tricks, but the guest judges, who were staying at a nearby hotel and could know nothing of the infiltration, would not mince words on the quality of their food. If they tasted the work of amateurs, they would say so, and there'd be a problem. *Bottom line:* The infiltration would only work if the terrorists were seamlessly integrated into the show.

Sara, Al-Asari, a couple of segment producers, and several of the masked terrorists met in the kitchen to figure it all out.

"Maybe we hide you and your men during the cooking challenges, then bring you back out right after?" suggested Sara.

"Oh, really," said Al-Asari. "And you certainly won't flag down security when our heads are turned?"

"What if you take part in the physical parts of the challenges, and then we swap you into vans during the cooking? That way you can watch without being detected," a segment producer suggested.

"Even worse. If the men at the checkpoint tower see even one masked man making a run for it, they'll shoot directly at the van," Al-Asari countered.

Sara sighed deeply and rubbed her temples. There was a sense of doom in the room, a mathematical equation that could not be solved. The terrorists sat around and waited.

"We need at least one cook with real skills," Sara said. "Either that or we hold off production and hope for the best until your helicopter comes."

"No, it must be business as usual," Al-Asari said. He threw up his hands in frustration. "There must be a solution."

"I can cook," said a quiet voice from the back of the room. It was one of the terrorists, a man so slight that his mask drooped over his shoulders.

"These chefs are classically trained, Salid," said Al-Asari. "Their skills cannot be faked."

"There would be no faking," replied Salid, softly.

"Don't make me lose my patience," Al-Asari said. "You will ruin everything with your foolishness. Now, what if we put..."

"I cooked for Mohamed Al-Shaeik," Salid said.

Al-Asari laughed scornfully. "Yes, yes, of course you cooked for Al-Shaeik. And I sang with Reem Kelani at Mahjar's!" All of the terrorists laughed now. "Enough with your stories, Salid. We have work to do."

"He came to my home to visit my mother when she was ill. They are from the same village," Salid continued. "His car was late in coming to pick him up so he dined with us. He said that I have a genuine gift."

"Salid is a *balaboosta*!" the largest terrorist, named Sheik, said. All the terrorists laughed, one slapping Salid on the back of the head.

"I swear it to be true," Salid muttered.

"What about your sisters?" said Al-Asari. "They do not cook?"

29

"My mother liked the taste of my food best. It made her feel at peace," said Salid.

"Fine," said Al-Asari. He pulled a chef's knife with a wooden handle from the block and grabbed an onion off the counter. "Show us."

"Yes, go ahead and be the wife," Sheik jeered.

Salid stood up and walked to the counter. He picked up the knife gently, took a deep breath, and closed his eyes. A lightning-fast flick of his wrist chopped off the ends of the onion, then turned it into a row of paper-thin slices in two seconds flat. The room went silent. Salid laid down the knife, returning to his seat on the floor next to the enormous Sheik.

Sara shrugged. "I guess we found our cook," she said.

"Seems we have," said Al-Asari.

"There's an area above the pavilion where we can hide the fake terrorists for now," Sara said. "But they must remain safe. None of this is their fault."

"Keep guns on them," Al-Asari instructed his men. "They try to run, shoot them. But otherwise, be steady."

Two terrorists walked out of the kitchen, guns in hand.

Another terrorist came running in. "Mr. Al-Asari. Pardon my interruption. We have problem," he said, breathless.

"Speak," said Al-Asari.

"The man with the gunshot wound and his wife."

"Yes, what is the problem?"

"They're trying to kill each other."

In a dingy but spacious supply closet, Warren Lopez slumped on the floor and winced as Ruti cleaned and bandaged his gunshot wound. Warren's wife, Sharon, paced the floor, making figure-eights with her cellphone in an effort to get at least one bar for cell service.

"The Wi-Fi in this place is dogshit," she said. "I told you this was going to happen. No tax credit is worth being offline when you have a family, Warren. So irresponsible."

"It wasn't my decision, Sharon... Ouch!"

"Stop moving," said Ruti, removing fragments of the bullet.

"What will happen to us, Warren? What will happen to Kale?" Sharon said.

Lopez winced again, this time at the sound of his adopted son's name. *Kale.* That she'd convinced him to give the boy such a ridiculous name was a testament to how much power she had over him.

"He'll be fine," he said. "Worse comes to worst, my sister will take care of him for a bit."

"Stephanie?" she said. "Are you on crack? She lets her four-year-old play *Gods of War* on PlayStation—no wonder he's on meds. And don't give me that line about educational apps—it's a slippery slope between some math game and zombie Nazi killers. If we die, Kale goes to my mother. She'll raise him the way I was raised. Look how I turned out."

Lopez looked over at her. "Over my dead body."

"All done," said Ruti, tucking away her supplies. "Keep it elevated. I'll change the bandages in a few hours. Truth is, you got very lucky."

"Wait," Lopez said. "Don't leave."

Ruti smiled sympathetically but headed for the door. A masked terrorist with an Uzi let Ruti out and locked the door behind them.

Sharon Lopez shot venom at her husband. "Did you cancel the credit cards yet, Warren?" she asked.

"Before or after getting shot?" said Lopez.

"Who knows what kind of scam they're running here," said

Sharon. "Do you know that fraud affects your credit score even if it's not your fault? And with the house on the market, that could mean thousands, no, tens of thousands of dollars thrown out the window, and all you do is sit there? Tell me, Warren, what are you doing to fix this problem, not to mention the dozens of other disasters that we're facing? And besides…"

Lopez took a deep meditative breath and tried to escape into the special place in his mind: a log cabin on Mammoth Lake with his college buddies—bong smoke in the cool, clean air, sizzling T-bones on the grill, and cold beer in alumni cups, laughing about some drunken frat house episode that ended poorly a thousand years ago.

"Okay already!" said Lopez, when it didn't work. "Stop! You haven't so much as said hello to me since you got here. And even for you, you're acting like a total . . ."

"What? A *cunt*, Warren? Don't you dare say it. You sound like your father again."

"Always bringing up my father…"

"He's a misogynist. And, I'm starting to see that you learned from him well."

"Is this about the Twitter thing?" Lopez ventured. "Because I've apologized a million different ways."

"You tweeted that we were getting a divorce, Warren."

"It was an April Fool's joke. People need a sense of humor!"

"It was March 29th. Three days early. Three days, Warren."

"My Blackberry calendar broke. We did couples therapy over this. Not to mention I lost hundreds of Twitter followers." Sharon shot lasers at him.

Lopez sighed. "You used to think my fuck-ups were charming."

"Right. Okay, here's a charming idea," said Sharon. "Next April, tweet that I've got cancer. Go ahead."

"You think that would fly?"

"Asshole."

"Kidding! Jesus! Just trying to lighten the mood," said Lopez.

"Then try having an adult conversation. Ever heard of those?"

Lopez scoffed. "Let me guess, because I can only think of one adult conversation with you. You want to talk about getting pregnant and giving Kale a sibling?" Sharon said nothing. "I've gone to how many clinics, Sharon? Six? Eight? I shoot blanks, okay. I smoked too much weed in college; I should never have worn tighty-whities. To be happy, do you need to emasculate me for the rest of my life?" Just to spite her, Warren picked up his cell phone, opened Sugar Rush, and squeezed in a quick game using his last three percent of battery power.

"I'm pregnant," Sharon said. "Fourteen weeks."

Lopez's fingers played one last line, a purple diamond triple that barely shifted the field, before his phone dropped in his lap.

"You don't seem excited," Sharon said.

"I-I-I'm... in shock," said Lopez. "Does this mean... I mean, are you saying... *I'm a breeder?*" A proud smile spread across Lopez's face. His fists clenched in victory, he raised them high.

"Warren..."

"I am The Golden Forebear! The Alpha! Hey, terrorist guy, get in here. I've got an announcement. I'm going to be a progenitor!"

"Warren..."

"I knew those tests were bullshit. I felt it. Don't get grossed out, but my load felt strong after drinking those protein shakes. I had one that Thursday after I played squash with Dave Bresdan. I bet that's the day..."

"Warren, it's not yours," said Sharon. "Well, it is but... I used a donor."

"You have to be shitting me."

"So it's not yours, genetically speaking. I would have told you but…"

Lopez went crimson. He spoke slowly, with a coiled rage. "We agreed that we wouldn't use a sperm bank. In therapy. On that fucking three-hundred-dollar-an-hour couch. You agreed."

"I didn't use a bank," Sharon said. "I used a… a direct donor."

"You did *what?*" Lopez said.

"Ryan Riffstein."

"Ryan Riffstein?" Warren found himself repeating the name, and then a flash of recognition lit his stunned eyes. "The dick doctor?"

"He's a well-respected urologist, and he was the only one to agree."

"You asked others?!"

"Not too many."

"You fucked my best friend," Warren said, in shock.

"You barely know him, Warren. Besides, I didn't sleep with him. He did it in a cup. Actually, it was your USC beer stein."

"You let Ryan Riffstein jizz in my alumni cup?"

"He did it mostly alone."

"I'll fucking kill him!" Lopez slammed his hand down on his leg and reeled from the pain. "Fuuuuuck!" he screamed.

The guard opened the door, gun first. "Quiet in here," he said.

"It's okay, Farkha. I just told him the baby's not his," said Sharon.

"Oh, okay," said the guard, lowering his gun.

"Wait. The terrorist knows?" Lopez said.

"I had to tell him I was pregnant. If my blood sugar drops, it could hurt the baby."

The terrorist gave Lopez a sympathetic shrug. Warren tried to laugh, but instead felt a great fury rise within him. He shot up from the ground and, with surprising force, lunged towards the terrorist. And he might just have knocked the guy on his ass had his cellphone, still paused on Sugar Rush, not gotten stuck underfoot, sending Warren splayed out onto his back, moaning in agony.

"What was that?" Sharon asked.

The terrorist shrugged again and closed the door on his way out.

The hot young chefs of *Natural Dish-aster: Season Five* arrived on set in a ten-passenger van, hung-over but in crisp chef whites. Several of the chefs had styled their hair into faux-hawks in tribute to the hospitilized Chef Brandon. In homage, Chef Etienne went so far as to tattoo a "B" for Brandon onto his already heavily inked forearm. Sara, Ruti, and Al-Asari sat in the control room tent with the DP awaiting the arrival of the terrorists.

"Send them in," Sara directed over walkie.

As had happened the previous day, three jeeps raced towards the docks packed with terrorists in black masks and red kafiya, armed with machine guns. The hot young chefs reacted seamlessly, sneering at and taunting the terrorists, calling them "fuckwads" and "douchebags." The terrorists jumped out of the Jeeps, machine guns across their chests. They stood on their marks.

"You think the chefs suspect anything?" Al-Asari said.

"They don't have the foggiest," replied Sara.

CJ Bazemore strutted out in a purple silk chef jacket with a dragon emblazoned on the back. "Team Amuse Bouche and Team Mise En Place, you have united to defeat the evil ISIS culinary terrorists," he said. "I will now only refer to you as one hybrid team—Team Mise En Bouche."

He paused for laughter. *Nothing.*

"Mise En Bouche, your teammate Chef Brandon has been kidnapped by these cray-cray Islamic fundamentalists and is now probably naked, undergoing who knows what kind of humiliation and torture. It will be your mission to get him back, and that means beating these terrorists in a series of culinary competitions."

A producer stepped in to goad the cast members. "Sneer at the terrorists with more energy, just not too much, and do it silently."

Bazemore continued, "Today's *Cannibal Challenge* goes back to the very basics of cooking: foraging. You will be collecting your main ingredients from the natural environment. Sound simple enough? Well, you don't know the half of it."

On the dock sat two mini-motorcycles as small as children's tricycles, but with the horsepower of Harleys. The docks were a serpentine obstacle course, with three coolers set up every fifty feet or so. At the final turn of the dock, several balloons covered in shaving cream were set up, and then farther still a thick rope dangled from a pole that leaned over the water's edge.

"A member of each team will drive a mini-moto around the track, grab their foraged ingredients from the coolers, shave two balloons, and then swing from that rope back to shore. Aside from a limited pantry, the ingredients you forage will be all your team will get to cook your dish, so choose well. And be quick, because the victorious team also wins a $5,000 gift certificate from Oakley's Beans. Oakley's Beans, the best beans in the business."

"Is that really the best you could do?" Ruti said in the control room.

"It's not about the challenge, it's about the human drama," explained Sara.

"No, I mean the integration. I figure every hummus house east of Bethlehem would want in on this show. Sabra, at least."

"Sabra wanted a verbal and an in-show usage integrated into every episode. Ad Sales said it would set a bad precedent."

The challenge was covered from every conceivable angle—

jibs, crisscross coverage, helmet GoPros shooting the face of the motorcyclists, and then an underwater camera in case there was a swimmer. Sara directed camera in Strider's stead, and the Director of Photography was on board.

CHEF COWBOY (INT.): "I really want to beat these ISIS bastards so we can save Chef Brandon... Plus, I could really use that five grand... from Oakley's Beans (frankenbite)... Their... beans are... delicious."

Both teams chose their shortest teammate to ride the mini-bike, and the two competitors lined up at the start of the dock. Chef Clora, a stunning Vietnamese chef whose Bahn Mi food truck once caused a riot in Austin, Texas, stood next to a man dressed head to toe in army fatigues and a black ski mask. Clora shot him a vicious side-eye.

CHEF CLORA (INT.): "So I'm on my bike, inches away from this crazy ISIS terrorist, and I'm like, 'Screw it. This clownhole's going down.'"

TERRORIST #4 (INT.): "The Infidel has a crazy look of calm on her face—the face of a martyr seconds before their bomb ignites... *Are you nuts—I'm not saying this!" (*trimmed in edit).

CJ Bazemore shot a pistol in the air and a flag came out that said "FORAGE!"

Clora revved her engine and sped across the narrow dock, cutting off the terrorist, who immediately fell over and injured his ankle. He moaned and lifted up the motorcycle, but Clora was already at the end of the dock collecting lentils, olive oil, apples, and pomegranates from the first cooler and throwing it all into her backpack. Back on her bike, she sped towards the next cooler.

The terrorist, dizzy from pain, fell again on the way down the dock and so, exasperated and desperate, he rolled the bike towards the first cooler. There he found only mayonnaise and dragon fruit, two ingredients that even he understood to be deadly in a culinary competition.

"Daughter of a donkey!*" the terrorist yelled (*additional audio added in post).

Clora grabbed oxtail and lamb chops from the protein cooler and drove on. When the terrorist arrived and found only eel and beef tongue, he cursed the heavens. Meanwhile, Clora was already past the final cooler and at the balloon station. She grabbed the first of the cream-covered balloons and shaved it like Capone's barber—careful and quick.

"You know how many dudes have let me shave their balls?" Clora called out triumphantly, wiping the last of the balloons clean. She fastened her backpack, leaned forward on her bike, and raced off the edge of the dock. The bike fell into the water just as she grabbed the rope and swung herself onto dry land, her premium ingredients intact and none the worse for wear.

The terrorist was not so fortunate.

CHEF LizZ (INT.): "He gave it his all, revving the engine hard, but at the last second, he totally pussied out and his bike bucked him off like a drunk dude on a mechanical bull."

The terrorist recovered mid-air and managed to grab the rope with one hand. But instead of swinging himself onto land, he shifted back to the dock, where his ribs hit hard and he fell into the water like a stone. When the medics rushed to the terrorist's aid, he waved them off and, in an angry fit of machismo, swam himself to shore with his now wet, totally shitty cooking ingredients.

"*Cha-ching* go the underwater cameras!" said the Line Producer, offering Sara a high-five.

"Giving the Network their money's worth," Sara grinned. "It's what we do." She flipped on her walkie. "Repo cameras for cooking."

Cooking stations were set up near the docks. A metal pantry rich with spices sat next to gas ranges and two long, metallic cooking stations. Both teams stood at the edge of the docks with their "foraged" groceries in-hand.

"On your marks … run!" shouted CJ Bazemore.

The fifty-yard dash provided Supertease fodder, and when Chef Nisha twisted her ankle on the way and sobbed real tears, the producers again high-fived.

Both teams laid out their foraged ingredients on their cooking stations and discussed their options. Salid was stunned by the paucity of choice—dragon fruit, eel, turnips, mayonnaise, peanuts, etc. At least they had zucchini and the beef tongue. He closed his eyes to think.

"We are ruined," a terrorist said.

"Salid, what do we do?" said another, seeing that Salid had closed his eyes. "He sleeps. What now?"

"Forget him," growled Sheik, who was built like an NFL lineman, and whose mask barely made it over his thickly muscled neck. "I will lead. We make babaganoush."

"But we have no eggplant."

"Shut up and listen to me." Sheik bared his teeth and the terrorist cowered. "Hand me the mayonnaise."

Al-Asari watched nervously in the control room. "Salid is choking. How can we hide this?"

"There's no stopping story," said Sara. "If Salid chokes, he chokes."

But Salid was not choking. He wasn't even there. He was far off in a childhood memory, recalling the day his father was arrested. Salid must have been six or seven years old at the time. The settlers had raided his town again. This time they had knives and sticks. They set fire to the olive groves, dousing the branches with gasoline. Several local men, including Salid's father, came with buckets of water to put out the fire, but also sticks and knives of their own, desperate to save their only means of income. But the men in white shirts, kippas, and tallits meant business.

There were younger ones too, children with them, and their bearded fathers cheered them on as they lit the olive branches. One young boy who was Salid's age wandered off into the groves with a red toy-truck on a string. When the string untethered, the boy sat down in the dirt and began to cry. Salid walked over. He took the string from the boy's hand and re-tethered it. They sat together in the dirt, amidst the smoke and screams and violence and played quietly with the truck, passing it back and forth.

"Yonatan!" a gruff voice called out in the grove. "Yonatan!" Fire licked the air around them and black smoke billowed in the sky. The two boys didn't even notice. "Yonatan!" the man called, closing in.

"Abba?" the little boy called out. When the man with the gruff voice and thick beard saw his son sitting in the dirt with Salid, he ripped him away as if from a sewer rat. "Do not speak with these people!" he said. "They are our enemy. Do you know the evil they have done? The killing?" His eyes burned with rage as he carried his boy away. "We must leave. It is dangerous now." The boy waved to Salid and threw his red truck down in the dirt for him to keep. Salid picked the truck up off the ground and waved back at the boy. And that's when the army came. Sirens everywhere, smoke bombs, the deafening thump of military helicopters. Salid ran straight home. When he got there, his mother was curled up on the floor weeping. His father was missing.

"He's a good man," she cried. "A peaceful man!"

Salid hugged her, trying to cushion his mother's agony, but she wept and wept. He couldn't believe the amount of tears. That night, after her crying had finally subsided, Salid's mother sat him down to a steaming plate of *sinaya*. Served in a terracotta bowl, it is a hearty Palestinian dish layered with tomato, fried zucchini, ground beef, pine nuts, and a thick helping of tahini.

"You are the man of the house now," his mother said. "You

must eat and grow strong."

Salid dove into the aromatic dish and his mother stroked his hair as the steam hit his face and the earthy flavors filled him. He ate and ate until his emotional pain gave way to stomach cramps, until there was only him and the food. His father was gone now. He didn't know for how long, or if he would ever return, but *sinaya…* that made him feel like he could survive.

"We make *sinaya*," Salid said, finally opening his eyes.

"He wakes," a terrorist mocked. "The midget chef wakes!"

"I will prepare the dragonfruit and the eel," said Salid. "Rahan and Farkah, dice onions and zucchini, as thin as you can. Mohammed, crush peanuts for tahini."

"*Sinaya?*" sneered Sheik. "That is peasant dish! We continue with babganoush. You have already failed us, Salid. It is over for you."

"Yes, we follow Sheik," a terrorist said. "But we still have no eggplant."

"Shut up and cook!" yelled Sheik.

Salid turned to the giant Sheik, a great resolve in his voice. "Sheik, you are a powerful man," he said. "Your strength is legendary. I respect you and your family. But this is my kitchen. I am in charge. And you will obey my command."

Salid peered up into Sheiks's eyes and did not blink. Sheik bared his teeth and turned a shade of red that was close to blood itself. The others thought Sheik might rip Salid's jugular out on the spot and add it to the babaganoush.

"It's your throat," Sheik growled.

Salid lit the gas ranges. "Tarik, I need you to squeeze the juice from these turnips," he said. "Ramin, crush the garlic to a pulp. Isham, boil salted water like the sea and squeeze in a full lemon, then cover. I'm going to get us through this, but we must move fast."

The men exchanged glances—they knew the sound of

authority when they heard it. Salid grabbed the eel and slit the skin just behind the gills, circled the body with his blade, and peeled it back. He then cut into the ventral opening and sliced into the membrane before discarding the guts—the filleted eel was clean and ready to cook. The terrorists fell in line. Salid gave orders, and even Sheik complied.

From the control room, Al-Asari shook his head. "So that's it? They plan a menu and cook. How do you make TV from this?"

"Wait for it," Sara said.

Across the way, Team Mise En Bouche rejoiced at the wealth of their ingredients—a chef's dream of lamb, oxtail, lentils, virgin olive oil, and more.

"We robbed a Whole Foods!" exclaimed Chef Nisha.

They all agreed that their ingredients were stellar, but with such an abundance of choices before them, the decorated young chefs of Team Mise En Bouche would have to actually agree on a menu plan. They huddled in a circle.

"Let's do an elevated Stampede pulled-pork mac and cheese," suggested Chef Dex, also known as "Cowboy," since he was from Texas and that sobriquet worked for Casting. He wore a ten-gallon cowboy hat to play it up.

"Pedestrian," sighed Chrissy, a vegan food blogger in hipster glasses who had scored a book deal after her celebrated Twitter feud with Paula Deen.

"How about a sage-infused hand-picked artisanal lamb shank steak with a maple mousseline and oregano-curried oxtail tartar with jalapeno aioli?" suggested Etienne, whose lumberjack beard and fully-tattooed forearms were compulsory in Portland kitchens.

"Why don't you just blow Alain Passard while you're at it?" said Tanya. "Can we all agree that we're going farm to table?"

"YES," everyone said.

"And that it should be some kind of elevated comfort food?"

"YES."

"I can use the bone marrow to start an offal app," said Chef LizZ, who spelled her name that way. Her severe buzz cut and Suicide Grrrls neck tattoo implied that the spelling was non-negotiable.

"No fucking offal, LizZ. Offal is Awful," said Chef Nisha.

"Guys, we're in Israel. Let's stay locavore," suggested Chef Ghana, who had left an investment banking job at Morgan Stanley to open Mrs. Nice, a popular East Village eatery featuring duck confit Jamaican patties. "We need to tell a story with this meal. Think about it—the story of Passover."

"An elevated Seder plate," said Tanya. "Genius."

"Too Jewish?"

"Let's add a Palestinian element," said Etienne "A stuffed vegetable *mahashi*?"

"Leave it to the French guy to add a dash of anti-Semitism," said Chef Cowboy.

"Salope putain!" said Etienne.

"I'll work on the shank bone."

"I'll devil the eggs with shaved truffles."

"I'll do pomegranate-glazed *charozet*."

"Twenty-two minutes left!" CJ Bazemore called out.

And just like that, the chefs got to work, with a focus and determination that seemed unimaginable seconds before.

CHEF GHANA (INT.): "We settled on an elevated Seder plate, which was an inspired idea if I do say so myself. It was nice to have the whole team onboard."

CHEF JOAQUIM (INT.): "The Seder plate idea is idiotic and slightly racist, but fuck it. This thing bombs, Ghana's the one getting thrown under the bus, not me."

CHEF CHRISSY (INT.): "As the youngest chef on the team, I'll read the four questions. Oh wait. All four questions are the same: 'What was Etienne thinking adding a Palestinian element to a Seder plate?' That dude is all ten plagues."

Back on the terrorists' side, Salid moved with the grace and strength of a Bolshoi dancer. He tossed spices in the air, twirled saucepans, chopped with laser precision, inhaled aromas, and nipped sauces from the tip of a wooden spoon as he solved an ever-evolving math problem to which he always knew the answer. The others stayed busy, tidying up when they weren't chopping or mixing under Salid's instruction. "Let it simmer," Salid said. "The key is patience."

"Four minutes left!" CJ Bazemore called out.

"He's incredible," Ruti said from the control room. "A natural talent."

"Definitely easy to watch," admitted Sara. "But he still has to face the judges."

With only a minute left, Salid Jackson-Pollacked his sauces into an artful crescent on the plates and delicately balanced crispy tarragon leaves atop. He used his last few seconds to size up Team Mise En Bouche. He saw their training, their precision, their determination, but he saw no passion in their work.

"That's it. Time's up," CJ Bazemore said, adding, "Put your hands in the ay-urr. I wanna see your armpit hay-urr!"

"We'll get that in pick-ups." Sara rolled her eyes.

"May I introduce our esteemed judges for this challenge," continued Bazemore. "Sir Philippe Duvall is the Chief Culinary Critic for the London Times."

A cravat-wearing bear of a man in a double-breasted suit and enormous gold cufflinks on his starched French cuffs nodded and frowned.

"And of course you all know author, social critic, international environmental activist, and former *Sports Illustrated* swimsuit cover girl, Bilha Tekeli," said Bazemore.

The Supermodel, who wore a dress two sizes smaller than a

Kleenex, gave her trademark sexy-face and coy wave.

Cameras were set for Team Mise En Bouche to present first. Chef Ghana walked the plates up to the judges' table.

"What we have here is a deconstructed Seder plate," she said. "A delicious shank bone of roast lamb encrusted with tarragon and a foam béchamel glaze, an oxtail *maror* liverwurst infused with date reduction, fried parsley spiced with local hand-picked lemon rinds, deviled eggs with *za'atar*, and tahini-infused *charoset*. We have also added a Palestinian element, *mahashi*, with braised prunes and pine nut puree. The Seder plate comes from a time when Israel lived in racial harmony, without walls, and Arabs were one with the Jews. Enjoy."

"That interpretation of history is completely insane," muttered Al-Asari in the control room.

The Cravat and the Supermodel picked up their forks. Bilha Tekeli dipped her fried parsley into kosher salt water and acted as she always did—as if she was full. She took a small sampling of the other elements and smiled when she tasted the *maror*. Duvall took bigger portions of everything, but he showed no emotion. His frown was immovable. Chef Ghana waited patiently, smiling and nodding.

"It eats well," the Cravat said. "Good mouth-feel on the shank bone. A competent deviled egg. And I was happy to see a genuine Palestinian *mahashi* on the Seder plate. Haven't seen that before."

"Thank you," Ghana gloated, but Duvall wasn't done.

"Your oxtail is woefully overcooked and your *charozet* is poorly seasoned. The apple went limp on my fork. Rather disappointing."

"Thank you," Ghana repeated, now stoic.

She turned her attention to Bilha Tekeli. "Passover has always been my favorite holiday, and *charozet* was always my favorite part growing up. I liked to swirl it around on my tongue and let the honey drip down my chin all sweet and sticky," said the Sports Illustrated cover model. "Unfortunately, this *charozet* lacked sweetness. And the oxtail, I agree, is dry. All in all, it's a well-executed plate but lacks the joy I recall as a little girl."

"Thank you," repeated Chef Ghana, bowing and looking to the ground. She returned to her team, who gave encouraging pats on the back.

"ISIS terrorists, please introduce your dish," said CJ Bazemore.

Sheik nudged Salid forward but he resisted.

"I cannot," Salid said.

"Now you are frightened?" Sheik grinned. "Then be frightened. Or I crush you."

He shoved Salid forward. The tiny chef found himself standing several feet from the judges' table with half a dozen cameras fixed on him. His entire body shuddered. He picked up the plates and walked them over to the judges, hands shaking as he laid them down. "This is a traditional comfort food called *sinaya*," he said, his voice barely audible.

"Speak up, boy," The Cravat said. "You're not this timid when you're murdering women and children in Libya, I bet."

Salid collected himself with a deep breath. He closed his eyes and thought back to what had inspired the dish.

The Cravat rolled his eyes. "Oh boy, we've got a real communicator here!"

Salid swallowed hard. His throat felt like sandpaper. He heard Sheik growl behind him, his hot breath nearly toppling him.

"My mother made me this dish at a time of great personal sadness," Salid said, louder now. "It made me feel like a human being again. It reminded me how rich life can be even when you have great sorrow. That is all you need to know." He bowed his head and waited.

"Acceptable description," the Supermodel said. "Let us taste."

The judges leaned forward, eager to scrutinize the plating of a dish that seemed a bit too—how could they put it?—a bit too Arab. But as they did, the sweet earthy aroma of the cumin, *za'atar*, and fried onions filled their nostrils, and their eyes closed blissfully.

There is a specific way that judges are supposed to eat a dish on-camera during a culinary competition. They are to look into the eyes of the chef and frown; they are to take a small forkful that contains many of the flavors; they are to chew lightly and dab the corners of their mouths after the bite, sip some water, and then frown, even if they are about to deliver good news. But something overcame both Philippe Duvall and Bilha Tekeli when the sumptuous aroma of Salid's cooking entered their nostrils. Something primal. They felt a hunger seldom arrived at during this age of quick service. An aching hunger. But not for food alone—for the simple joy of being alive. The scent triggered a memory back to their happiest, simplest days, surrounded by family and friends, stifling belly laughs and tears at a beautiful story well told.

Reflexively, their forks contained a much larger portion than was permitted, and when the *sinaya* touched their tongues, they abandoned any sense of poker face and all but foodgasmed for the cameras. The sexiest woman in Israel and possibly the world moaned audibly. She repositioned her thighs in a way that made the Cravat look over for only a split second before using that disruption as an opportunity to take a second forkful of Salid's dish. No one takes a second forkful. Not ever.

The Supermodel actually bent over and licked the plate clean of its sauces, a sight that many men and women on the crew leaned in to behold. The two judges had just completely lost themselves.

"Please remind the talent that these are the bad guys," Sara said over walkie.

A producer awoke the two judges from their daydream. The Supermodel and The Cravat were irritated by the interruption. Their instinct was to cry out like newborn babies pulled too soon from the warmth of the womb.

The Cravat gazed at Salid, confused and suspicious, his eyes wet, his mouth unable to be utilized for anything but culinary pleasure. The Supermodel ran a finger slowly along her pouty lips to extend the tingling sensation she felt there.

Sara peeked her head out of the control room tent and called out impatiently, "So, how was it, Judges?"

"It was nothing short of brilliant," the Cravat said in breathless amazement. His face was painted in genuine gratitude.

"The sun, the moon, the stars," the Supermodel moaned. "The ocean, the valleys, the mountains ..."

"Brilliant," said The Cravat. "Bravo, young man. What you have created here is a unicorn in the culinary realm. A true *chupacabra*."

"My body is tingling everywhere," said Tekeli.

There was a pause in production as Sara spoke into the Judge's earpieces. "Hey, gang, so that was great—exactly what was needed. We're just going to want some negatives to even this out or else it won't cut right."

"Got it," Philippe Duvall said, forcing a frown and trying to pull himself together.

"Some negatives, of course," said Tekeli, straightening her miniskirt. The Supermodel looked in her compact mirror and applied some lipstick, a brighter shade of red than before. She looked in Salid's general direction without looking at him directly.

"Candied dates? That's a bit, um, derivative," she coughed out, embarrassed by the insincerity of her words. "Yes, I've seen that before. It's not terribly new, is it?"

"New?" Salid said.

"Absolutely not new whatsoever," the Cravat cut in, thankful to have something to build on. "And the dish was a bit too, um, well, too little of it, frankly." The Cravat looked down his nose at a plate all but licked clean. "Not nearly enough food overall. I mean, do you wish me to starve, sir?" he said with more resolve. "No, this would never make it out of my kitchen. My readers would be left wanting more. So very much more."

"Precisely," said the Supermodel. "There simply wasn't enough food on the plate to eat. Terribly disappointing, that."

Having never experienced criticism of his cooking, let alone from two internationally known food personalities, Salid genuinely felt hurt. "Thank you," he managed, head bowed deeply.

"No, thank you, young man," said the Cravat.

"Repo cameras for the announcement," said the 2nd AD.

Sara headed out of the control room tent. Her next bit of business would require a light touch. She weighed her words carefully as she walked towards the talent.

Philippe Duvall and Bilha Tekeli stood by the Crafty Table sharing a single cigarette.

"Pretty close one," Sara said, pulling out a cigarette of her own.

Both judges were aghast. "You still smoke those things?" the Supermodel said.

"Aren't you afraid of cancer?" asked Duvall.

"But..."

"This?" Bilha said, looking at the cigarette she was smoking like it was something else entirely. "This is post-coital. Did you taste that dish? The boy is a master. Tell me, who did he train with? Chef Ottolenghi? Scheft? Shaya?"

"I see the world in a deeper way now," marveled Duvall. He took the cigarette from Tekeli and lifted it to his lips. "It's really about human love and kindness, isn't it? That bond."

"Yes, love. And mothers. And family," Tekeli said, gazing off into the sky.

Sara was losing ground, so she ripped off the bandage. "It would really help if you gave this one to Team Mise En Bouche," she said. "This is a sponsored challenge, and I don't know how Oakley's Beans would take it if the terrorists won."

"Absolutely not," said the Cravat. "If the terrorists lose, I walk."

"Ditto," said the Supermodel.

"I hear you," Sara said. "And we should build on that. My concern is we'll look to be pandering. This episode will air around Holocaust Remembrance Day. We may appear to be sympathetic to a sworn enemy of Israel and America. I mean, they should win, but just not this round, okay?"

"Absolutely this round," insisted the Cravat. "Screw Oakley's Beans. They sell chemical-infused sludge."

"From your lips to Hashem's ears," says Bilha. "By the way, couldn't you have gotten a hummus sponsor? Sabra should have been all over this."

Sara smiled, considering her next move. "Philippe, may I please have a word? About something else entirely."

"Certainly. But I won't change my mind. I assure you of that," Duvall said. He handed the supermodel the cigarette. "Excuse me, Madame Tekeli."

"Stay strong," she said. "Sara is a snake in the Garden of Eden."

"Agreed."

Sara walked off with Duvall, who was already ranting. "I absolutely will not bend on this one. Feel free to send me packing. I have my integrity, and integrity cannot be bought."

"I read your article in the Times," said Sara. "I had no idea you were such a fan of Chef Hung Mhamia."

"The man is my gastronomic god. His *bimbombap* is from heaven," said Duvall. "But that's in my bio. What kind of snake oil are you selling, Sara? Because I'm not buying."

"What if I could get Chef Mhamia to blurb your new book?" said Sara.

Duvall scoffed. "Mhamia never blurbs," he said. "That's part of his mystique and, frankly, something that I respect deeply about him. A man of his talents and integrity wouldn't shuck his name off like that. His brand is purity, earthliness. He cooks and eats only the cleanest farm-to-table herbs and plants. His fish are imported straight from the Sea of Jumpai."

Sara pulled out her iPhone and flipped on her video app. On the small screen was a video of Chef Hung Mahamia sitting on a hotel bed. He had a bottle of Wild Turkey on one knee and a giggly brunette in a low-cut miniskirt on the other. Mahamia leaned forward, causing the camera to jerk and revealing that Sara was the one filming.

"You know Chef Mahamia?" Duvall was shocked.

"Wait for it," said Sara.

The camera panned back to Mhamia. He pushed the brunette off his lap and grabbed an enormous bag painted with the Wok & Roll logo. "Fuck cooking," slurred the great chef. "This place serves delicious shit!" He dipped his hand into the bag and gorged on a greasy eggroll.

"An egg roll?" Duvall gasped, clutching his cravat. "Mhamia detests eggrolls. He calls them the French fries of Asia."

"Fucking delicious!" Mhamia laughed in the video. "Sara, stop hogging that General Tso's chicken. You know, I make the same shitty recipe at Ahusa House in London and call it *Kokaha-musai*. Philippe Duvall gave me five stars for it in that ridiculous rag he writes for. Ha ha ha!"

And then the video cut out.

Sara tucked the phone back into her pocket. "It's prearranged," said Sara. "I erase the video, he writes a lovely blurb for your book. His first. I can show you the text correspondence."

Duvall looked dazed. His forehead glistened with sweat and his upper lip trembled. "The terrorists must lose," he said, hypnotized. "I know that now."

"What about Bilha?" Sara said. "How will you convince her to go along?"

"I'll deal with her. Don't you worry," said Duvall. "You just get me that blurb."

Duvall walked off, speaking loudly enough for the Supermodel to hear. "I won't hear another word of it, Sara. The terrorists lose, we walk, and that's bloody final!"

"Bravo!" Tekeli called out. "My hero."

Duvall turned to Sara and mouthed: "Get me that blurb."

Sara nodded and headed back to the control room with a grin.

"We have our winners," CJ Bazemore announced. "The Cannibal Challenge goes to…" He pulled a card from the pocket of his silk chef coat. "Team Mise En Bouche! You are now one step closer to saving Chef Brandon's life and defeating the evil ISIS terrorists. Plus, you win a $5,000 prize from Oakley's Beans. Oakley's Beans, the best beans in the business."

The cast hooted and hugged. Sheik growled into Salid's ear. "I thought you said you can cook. You lost to dog food."

"It can't be," Salid said. "The dish was perfect."

"The judges don't agree apparently," Sheik said.

Bilha Tekeli convulsed when she heard the announcement. She turned to Duvall, and was shocked to see him looking coolly detached.

"You sold us out," she seethed at her co-judge. "What did Sara promise you? Tell me now, you greedy son of a bitch." She grabbed her purse and stood up, but Duvall steadied her, gently sitting her back down. "What are you doing?" Bilha hissed. "This is a travesty!"

"Wait for it," whispered Duvall.

"For what? You fucking sold us out," said Tekeli.

"I also want to announce an additional, more spiritual victory for Team Mise En Bouche," CJ Bazemore said. "On top of your winnings, an additional $5,000 from Oakley's Beans will be donated in your name to a charity very special to our esteemed judge Bilha Tekeli: the East Jerusalem Orphaned Animal Shelter."

All cameras pointed to Bilha, who quickly flipped her frown and blew a kiss to the winning team.

"Bravo, Mise En Bouche," she said in her thespian best. "The orphaned animals thank you."

Mise En Bouche celebrated with more hugs and hooting.

Duvall turned to Bilha. "Everything copacetic?"

"What's important is the orphans," Tekeli said.

After the announcement, the plan was to shoot fallout reality back at the Cast Mansion and then think of an excuse to bring over the terrorists. But a genuine in-the-moment reality scene broke out when Chef Clora walked off from her celebrating team and approached the terrorists all by herself.

"We've got a runner," Sara said into walkie. "Get there quick."

The cast members watched in shock as Clora engaged with the enemy.

"Hi, I'm Clora," she said to the row of masked men. "Look, we're all chefs here, no matter what we do in our free time. So why don't you guys come hang out at the cast house tonight? In fact, you should stay with us—there's plenty of extra beds and towels."

"Clora, what the heck!?" shouted Cowboy.

"Those guys murder children," Joaquim reminded her.

"So does peanut butter," Clora fired back.

CHEF ETIENNE (INT.): "The terrorists are standing there, sulking like petite bitches, when Clora invites them all to the house to chill out. I guess it was pretty cool of her."

CHEF COWBOY (INT.): "Are you fucking kidding me? I'm not having those dirt bags anywhere near my sweet Clora. This means war."

CHEF TANYA (INT.): "Who knows? Once we get those masks off, one of them might be cute."

The cast mansion was sick. Located eleven miles off the main beach in the Almog Hills, the fourteen-room seaside palace featured indoor/outdoor hot tubs, a fully stocked tiki bar, a hookah lounge equipped with a 108-inch LCD screen, ping pong and billiard tables, Sonos speakers, and bidets in all the bathrooms. Not to mention a view of the Gulf of Aqaba from all three balconies. Rumor had it Cat Stevens found Islam while doing K on the upper veranda.

The cast spent most of their time at the mansion tanning, drinking, and either fighting, or screwing in the open air, or pulling pranks. The newest prank was waiting until someone fell asleep and then duct-taping their butt cheeks together. Although the cast members were too young to recall the famed "Breakfast Club" reference, they'd heard about it and thought it was rad.

The only respite from hedonism was when the producers needed scenes to happen. On this particular evening, Clora needed to confront Tanya about hooking up with Brandon before he got kidnapped. It was an important story-beat to grab because extra footage of the season-long rivalry between Clora and Tanya had been requested by the Network. So they needed it. After that, the girls could go back to whatever the hell they wanted to do.

The scene was set at the lower hot tub. They wanted a slow burn scene: Tanya would be sitting there reading a magazine and Clora would say she wanted to talk to her in private. Clora would say how meaningful Brandon was to her as an ex-boyfriend and how hurt she was when she found out Tanya had hooked up with him without asking how she felt about it. She would ask how serious it was between Brandon and Tanya. Then there would be tears and anger but ultimately a reconciliation that centered on concern for Brandon's life as a prisoner of evil fundamentalist terrorists. Post would love to flashback to Brandon's fall and kidnapping during the Jugular Challenge, so if the producers could make them talk about that, even better.

Cameras were up. Tanya sat by the hot tub and Clora walked over, arms crossed just as planned.

"Tanya, we should talk," she said.

"Um, okay, Clora. What about?"

Clora began, but out of the corner of her eye noticed a van pulling up to the mansion gates. It was packed with the terrorists from the challenge. Clora considered the terrorists her domain. She was the one who had invited them over, and she'd be damned if one of the other chefs was going to steal the scene when they arrived.

"Uh, I just . . . it's about, what I wanted to say..." Clora grabbed a drink off the edge of the hot tub and tossed it in Tanya's face. Then she pounced on top of her, grabbing her hair with both hands. Goodbye slow-burn scene. "You fucked my man and now he's kidnapped!" screamed Clora.

"He wasn't even yours!" Tanya yelled.

They rolled on the floor clawing at each other and pulling hair. Some other cast members broke it up.

"You can have him!" Tanya screamed. "He's clingy as shit and his balls are weird."

Clora got up, straightened her hair, and turned to the Producer: "You got it?"

"Pretty much," the Producer said, shrugging.

"You fucked up my hair," Tanya complained. "Now I gotta get all pretty for ISIS or whatever."

"Not if I get to them first," said Clora.

Nine men in black ski masks filed into the reality TV mansion carrying army rucksacks and machine guns.

"Glad you made it," said Clora, twisting her wrist around a glass of Pinot. "Allow me to show you to the boudoir."

Clora led the masked men to their quarters: a Pee Wee's Playhouse-themed funhouse with bunk beds that looked and smelled like strawberry chewing gum.

TERRORIST #7 (INT.): "The room was so gay it made *Behind the Candelabra* seem like *Die Hard* ... *What does that even mean?" (*trimmed in edit).

The terrorists showered up, and put on fresh kafiyahs and ski masks that had been cleaned, starched, and pressed by the production team. When they came up for food, the cast of *Natural Dish-aster* was waiting for them, standing in a row with their arms crossed and looking a bit sinister. For a moment, the whole thing looked like a trap. The terrorists clutched their guns, ready to engage, when Chrissy raised her beer.

"As a blogger transitioning to mainstream print, I understand your struggle for self-determination," she said. "While as a group we may disagree with your methods, in a way, we get it."

"Tonight, let's put all that aside," Chef Joaquim stepped in. "We're all cooks here. We care about the food. Am I right?" The terrorists said nothing. "Right. We're all just cooks, grinding it out behind the line, loving the adrenaline of a dinner rush, getting tattoos, doing coke in the pantry. Anyway, tomorrow we may be back to being mortal enemies, but tonight... we party."

"Yeah!" The cast members hooted, raising their glasses. *Time of Our Lives* by Pitbull and Ne-yo came on out of nowhere. The terrorists flinched as all the chefs besieged them with hugs and pats on the back. Cowboy even handed one of them a beer.

"Our religion forbids it," said one terrorist, causing a record-scratch type silence. Cowboy looked as if he didn't understand.

"Of course," Chef Ghana said, a glimmer of cultural sensitivity lighting her eyes. "How rude of us. And that's exactly why we brought a little gift." She raised a Ziploc bag filled with pink and green pills.

"Go pills! Go pills! Go pills! Go pills!" the cast members sang in unison and then collapsed in laughter as the music blasted back on.

Minutes later, terrorists and cast members alike lounged on couches playing Xbox. Spliffs were lit; ski-hill-sized rails were chopped on bathroom sinks. A blur of sticky pink drinks and raucous laughter took over.

Audio caught tidbits:

"So, are you guys like part of some community theatre troupe?" // "Ha! Tanya, this guy said he got his ink in an Israeli prison. I call bullshit!" // "Do you guys watch *Homeland?* Oh my God, you have to. It's all Islamic terrorists, but like crazy Islamic terrorists, not like you." // "Check out my dazzling Ahmadinejad iPhone cover! Are you so into it?" // "If you can snort that whole long rail, I'll totally flash you my tits!" // "DRINK! DRINK! DRINK!" // "Dude, let's blindfold wrestle. C'mon! I thought you were tough. You're a pussy!... Shit, dude, are you okay? I think I have your tooth. Ha! Ha!" // "Let's see how many of us can fit in the hot tub at once." // "NAKED PARTY!" // "I'm Mormon; it's been really hard." // "I'm Roman Catholic; it's been really hard." // "My dad is so fucking rich; it's been really hard." // "Do you have any idea what it's like to be half-black, half-Vietnamese in Texas?" // "I tried to commit suicide. Twelve times."

// "I was the only four-year-old in rehab." // "You guys are straight, right? If you kiss, I'll let you watch while I give Nisha a lap dance." // "I've had this erection so long I think I'm going to get gangrene!" // "Where did all those hash brownies go? You did? Uh… you'll be fine." // "What time is it anyway? (in unison): FOUR TWENTY! FUCK YEAH!" // "Get it? An 'axehole' is a guy who is an asshole who wears too much Axe body spray."

"Yeah, that's already a thing.

"I'm thinking of writing like a *Fifty Shades of Grey* for guys with small dicks. In like six months, well-hung guys are going to be growing their bush just to compensate." // "A little too close to home, dude."

"Yeah, that's awkweird. Ha, awkweird! That should be a thing!"

"It is." // I hate when people call Trump 'Cheeto,' because I always loved Cheetos. Flamin' Hots are my everything…"

"Ain't nothing wrong with President Trump neither…" "Shut it, Cowboy." // "And that, my friends, was what I call a Butt-Cheek Bieber." // "If we kiss, will you guys kiss?" // "Dude, I just got booked at UCLA to talk about my celibacy oath. Five grand. Aren't you there doing a sobriety panel? Dude, we should totally hook up, get shitfaced, and bone some freshmen." // "Cowboy's gonna wax his chode on camera!"

Ruti sat in the control room with Sara watching it all like some anthropology experiment. "Do these idiots ever sleep?" Ruti said.

"Most of 'em are in their twenties," Sara said. "Sleep is an inconvenience."

"What's happening now?" Al-Asari said, waking from a nap.

"Still partying," Ruti said.

"How is it possible?" said Al-Asari.

"It's what they do best."

Sara peeked at a text from her brother Nathan: "Tattooed guys came again. I hid like u said. When r u coming home?"

Sara wrote back: "Soon, buddy. Emergency phrase?"

Nathan: "Chasing Pavement is the worst song ever written. ☹"

Sara: "Good. Go to bed. Love you."

"Luv u, Minecraft ☺," wrote Nathan.

In the kitchen, Etienne sat at a table reading Balzac's *La Rabouilleuse* and frowning. Chef LizZ went to the fridge and poured herself some ginger ale, then added some cubes.

"Not in the partying mood, huh?" she said to the sulking Frenchman. "I heard someone's waxing their chode. That oughta be a blast."

"Children bore me," Etienne pouted, without looking up from his book. "They know nothing of culture."

"Renaissance man, huh? Hence the door-stop-of-a-book?"

"Just European. We don't need to act like petite imbeciles to feel joy."

LizZ sat across from Etienne and smiled. "For me, it's the program," she said, and took a sip of her ginger ale. "Thirty-three months clean today, thank you very much."

"*Mazel tov,*" said Etienne, uninterested.

"Still, I did love my junk," LizZ went on. "All of it. To this day, I wish to God I could just lose myself in a book or something like you're doing. Sometimes when I cook, it starts to happen. That voice disappears, but most of the time it's shouting in my ear to cop some."

"You have voices in your head?" Etienne grinned.

"All the time," LizZ smiled. "I try to focus on getting through each moment, you know. But yeah, the junkie in me is a real blabbermouth."

Etienne folded his book. He looked both ways to make sure no one was listening. "It speaks to me too," he admitted, finally

59

looking up at LizZ. She was surprised to see that his eyes were wet. "I feel weak most of the time. And the bastard just laughs at me, like he knows I'm going to fall off."

"I got you," said LizZ. She took Etienne's hand. "Look at us, right? A couple of Anthony Bourdains: cool, even after we kick?" She grinned. "You know who I pretended to be when I was high? Anne Burrell. Fucking Invincible Anne Burrell, with her corny blonde hair and sparkle tattoos, if you can believe that shit."

"I was Ludo," said Etienne. "Master of the fuck-you stare. Now I sweat when I talk. I feel like a nervous wreck most of the time."

"I know."

The two chefs sat there for a minute in silence.

"Let's cook something," said Etienne. "Together."

"Whoa! Hold up. The lone wolf wants to collaborate? You sure you're not high?"

"Let's make something that reminds us of what it's like," said Etienne. "That feeling."

"I'll grab the butter," said LizZ.

"Skip it. Duck lard," said Etienne.

"Oh, you *are* one sick-ass junkie."

Away from the cameras, which were covering an epic beer-pong battle, Tanya stumbled around the mansion grounds, a quarter bottle of Café Patron in her hand, searching for where all the action was. She staggered out to the back garden and spotted one of the terrorists. He sat cross-legged next to a palm tree, lit softly by the moon. He wrote in a small journal, scribbling notes, scratching them out, then scribbling some more. His ski mask was pulled up over his forehead, revealing full lips and soft, youthful cheeks. Tanya kicked a pebble and the terrorist fumbled to get his mask back on.

"Too late, Habib. I already saw you," said Tanya. "I could describe you to the authorities with a pot lolli in my mouth. You're pretty young for a bad guy, aren't you? Like a kid?"

"I'm a man," the boy said, forcing his voice low. "I have many wives."

Tanya walked up to him, plucked the mask off his head, and hurled it into a tree.

"Hey!" the terrorist said.

"Relax, David Foster Wallace," said Tanya. "I won't turn you in. You're too cute." She sat across from him, settling the bottle of Patron on her lap. "You working on some kind of suicide bomber manifesto?" she said.

The terrorist frowned.

"Just kidding! Jesus, I never heard of a sensitive terrorist. What's your name anyway?"

"Ramin," the boy said, then immediately regretted it.

"Whatcha writing, Ramin?" Tanya leaned over to peek. "Short, even lines, huh? Looks like poetry to me." She lay down on her side, allowing the full moon to light her. "Well, what are you waiting for? Read a pretty girl a poem."

"It's not nearly finished." Ramin squirmed. "I wouldn't feel comfortable."

"Oh, don't be a wuss," Tanya said. "I get poets. When I was on tour with Def Jam, I made out with Common." She flashed her bright blue eyes and leaned in. "Honey, sometimes in life, you gotta step up, and this is one of those times. I mean, look at the moon. The moon is begging to hear some poetry."

"It's not polished," Ramin muttered.

"Boring! Gawd, don't they teach you about women in Islamic summer camp? We like confidence. Even false confidence works."

"Okay," the boy said. "But you can't laugh."

"Scouts' honor," Tanya said, giving the Star Trek sign.

Ramin took a deep breath, exhaled slowly, and peered down at his journal. "A coral bouquet shakes in my sweaty palms," he read, voice quavering. "I pull the mermaid's chair and inhale her sea urchin perfume. 'That's sweet,' the mermaid says, accepting the flowers, 'but this still isn't a date. You're a fish, I'm a mermaid.' 'It's not unheard of,' I say. But she says 'This is just a favor to my Aunt Farrha.' She brushes her flowing golden hair to the side and puckers her pillowy lips.

"The waiter arrives with our food. 'See,' she says, pointing to my plate of worms. She slices greedily into her tilapia entrée. I look away. I knew the tilapia from high school drama class. 'Your eyes are luminescent,' I say and, despite myself, pop a worm in my mouth. She smiles. 'You're cute.' I feel hope in my heart, as if anything is possible if you are brave and true. Then a massive hook impales my face and I am lifted out of my chair and through the roof of the restaurant.

"The pain is excruciating. 'Be right back!' I manage as the Mermaid looks up in horror. I ascend through the murky water, tugged by the hook; up, up, up and out of the water into the horrible hot air. The sun burns my eyes. The oxygen suffocates me. I flop in the hands of a ghoulish pink giant, gasping for breath.

"The giant smiles at me with horrible teeth, shows me off to a smaller giant, then rips the hook savagely from my face, leaving a gruesome hole. Death is near, but all I can think of is how I stiffed the Mermaid with the restaurant bill. How embarrassing. Should have prepaid. Life escapes me. Breathlessness. Weightlessness. Emptiness. White light and cool calm, and then... SPLASH! Cold water surrounds me again and I breathe!

"I'm alive! I swim down into the depths as fast as I can but catch my reflection on a silver minnow and behold my deformity. My face is a mangled mess. When I reach the restaurant, the mermaid is sobbing, but the waiter, a handsome merman with golden hair and a square, manly jaw, is soothing her.

"My Mermaid wipes tears from her face, looks up at the merman, and leans into his muscular chest. I imagine pulling them apart, staking my claim as her man, telling her that I love her, proposing right there. I've got the ring and everything. But that cannot be. It is just a fantasy for a fish like me—a fish filled to the gills with cowardice. Then there's my deformed face to deal with. Still, it is a wonderful fantasy. A fantasy so delicious that I gorge on it for miles, as I swim away to the East, the loneliest fish in all of the Red Sea."

The boy folded his journal and breathed deeply. He looked up. Tanya lay on her side before him, lit by the brilliant moonlight. She snored peacefully, eyes closed and mouth slightly open.

Ramin sighed. He removed the bottle from Tanya's hands and covered her with his blanket.

"Goodnight, my Mermaid," he said, and walked off.

CHAPTER 4

The morning sun rose gently above the hills of the cast mansion, revealing a true natural "dish-aster"—empty tequila bottles piled in fallen pyramids, shards of broken glass swimming in puddles of dirty bong water, vomit speckling the bushes, and half-clothed bodies strewn all over the place, either curled up on couches, or splayed out on the billiards table, or face down on the floor.

Every kind of sin-tinged odor assaulted Sara's olfactory glands as she cracked open the mansion's control room door. Cigarettes, booze, and sex dominated the bouquet, though there were more sinister undertones. The terrorists, to their credit, had mostly crashed out in their Pee Wee Herman quarters, sleeping off the most confusing night of their lives. Several of them had peeled off their masks, and one was completely naked.

Sara tiptoed past the snoozing cast and crept into the kitchen. She brewed herself some Nescafe and flipped on the TV to local Israeli news. Her first treasured sip reminded her of the sensation she felt after completing night watch at base camp in Syria many years before—a sweet release after hours of tension and boredom.

On the TV, the newscaster switched from weather to local news. Mal-Malaika was still on the run from authorities, the newscaster said. A black and white surveillance photo came up on-screen—masked men in a getaway truck. A man with rimmed glasses and a graying moustache sat in the passenger's seat. His hand bore a big bandage speckled with blood. The newscaster said that this group was behind a terror attack that had killed seven, including two children. Sara took a long sip of her coffee.

"They always catch my ugly side," Al-Asari said, his voice breaking Sara's solitude. He pulled a mug off the shelf and poured himself a coffee. "To every face there is ugliness and beauty, just as to every story there is truth and lies. But every time I see a photo of myself, they only catch the ugly."

"And what about truth and lies? Which is it in this case?" said Sara.

"Complicated," said Al-Asari.

"Not for the seven dead," said Sara.

"True," said Al-Asari. He took a long sip of coffee and exhaled pleasure. "There is no gray area for the dead. Only blackness. But we are part of the living, aren't we, Ms. Sinek? Or forgive me, should I call you by your company name, Sergeant Sinek of IDF's One Hundred Seventy-Third Battalion? Tell me about the women and children you killed when you raided Jabalia all those years ago. Was that complicated as well?"

Sara stiffened at the mention of her IDF battalion and that fatal day in Jabalia. She gripped her mug tightly.

"Yes, yes, I know of you, Sergeant," Al-Asari smiled. "I know all about what your battalion did. We have more in common than you may think."

"We have nothing in common," Sara said through gritted teeth.

"Oh but we do. Because I do not know of Jabalia by chance. You see, it was my hometown. That fateful day your tanks rolled in changed my life too."

"I don't know what you're talking about," said Sara.

"Before that, I was something of a firebrand," Al-Asari said.

"Living in Gaza was impossible for my family—there were curfews, aggression from the police, midnight interrogations where my brothers would come back beaten to a pulp. I wanted revolution, and I had a chip on my shoulder. And yes, there was a girl I wanted to impress. What can I say? I was young—still stupid in many ways. So I joined a group of bad men one day. They told me we were going to steal computers in Tel Aviv and sell them for money to rebuild the town hospital.

"I was so naïve I didn't even know what I'd gotten myself into until the bomb went off. It was at the university. In the smoke and rubble and amidst all the screaming students, I swore I would dedicate myself to peace from that moment on, no matter what," said Al-Asari. "When I returned home weeks later, Jabalia was in ruins—the work of your battalion. A horrible mess of blood, broken glass, and homes razed to the ground. I found the girl I was trying to impress clinging to her dead brother. She had come unwired and I could no longer reach her.

"But he was not the only one killed. Your battalion hadn't counted on an Israeli being there, had you? A visitor from right here in Eilat—a hotel manager looking to hire Palestinian staff? You didn't count on him being in the apartment you shelled. Isn't that right, Sergeant Sinek?"

Sara glared at Al-Asari, her mouth tense and frowning.

Al-Asari grinned. "While my brothers plotted revenge, I kept my word to Allah. I turned to books, taught literature—went straight. And you . . . you turned to reality TV production. Both of us found solace in stories. Far better than our truth. Our guilt. And how ironic that we end up here, the two of us." Al-Asari moved closer to Sara. Inches separated their faces. "Tell me, Ms. Sinek, while you were playing lover girl with Ruti, did you mention to her that your tank was the one that shelled the apartment where her father was killed? That you were directly responsible for his death? Or did you leave that little tidbit out?"

Sara grabbed Al-Asari's throat and raised her fist to strike him.

"What is it, Ms. Sinek?" strained Al-Asari. "Does it hurt to have someone know who you really are? The horrors you are responsible for? That can never go away…"

Sara tightened her grip. She aimed her fist to kill, to squash Al-Asari, to kill the memory and the pain.

"Now, children," Ruti said. She walked casually into the kitchen, yawning. "Enough with the posturing. It's much too early for that."

Sara released Al-Asari's neck. He fell into a chair, coughing violently and gasping for breath.

"We were just… talking," said Sara, tightly.

"Yes," Al-Asari wheezed. "A couple of old friends sipping coffee and planning their day."

"Glad to hear it," said Ruti, pouring herself a coffee. "Because we've got a production schedule to keep. And I am severely under-caffeinated."

CHAPTER 5

Twenty-four hours of uninterrupted silence in a supply closet? Lopez couldn't recall if he'd ever spent even a handful of uninterrupted hours alone with his wife without at least the distraction of a glowing screen or cell phone calls. Regardless, he hadn't said a word since Sharon revealed to him that she was pregnant with Ryan Riffstein's dork sperm.

The news had stunned him and, as the waking hours passed, Lopez simply couldn't think of anything to say. He had immersed himself in his special place, and when that wore off, he thought about Kale. When they first adopted him, it was unadulterated joy. They drove to Griffith Park, laid out a blanket under the sun, ate cold grapes from a wooden bowl, and got used to the quaint horror of diaper changing.

Sharon was then so happy obsessing over the baby's every move. She slathered him with expensive sun block, tousled his surprisingly thick black hair, and sniffed the top of his head, calling it "hits off the butterscotch."

Warren and Sharon held hands and just stared at this little miracle from the Silverlake Interfaith Adoption Agency as he sucked on a non-toxic pacifier and played with a monkey doll that cackled when its belly was touched. And when Kale smiled his sly, crooked, knowing smile, Lopez and his wife toppled over in bliss. It was the start of something wonderful.

And it wasn't about them. It was about Kale, loving Kale, building his confidence, his intelligence so that the world would be anything he wanted. "The kid's insatiable," Lopez said, mixing another bottle of formula. "He comes from good, solid stock. Isn't that right, Mr. Kooky?"

"I love him so much," Sharon said. Then she smiled, a mischievous twinkle in her eyes. "Hey, you," she said. "Let's give him a sibling, okay? Tonight?" Sharon leaned in and joyfully kissed Lopez on the lips, her eyes shut in bliss.

But for Lopez, the kiss stung. All he could think was, *Why ruin a perfect moment? Why ask for more?* And it was then that Lopez understood his fate. He should have known ages ago. Due to his emasculatingly low sperm count, Lopez could never give his wife what she really wanted: a baby growing in her own belly. There would always be something missing in their marriage, even on a perfect sunny day in the park like this. Kale would feel it later in life, be hurt by it, and turn out just like all the other people Lopez knew—slightly sad and somewhat lonely but with no idea as to where those feelings came from.

Lopez awoke from his bittersweet reverie and shifted his aching foot. He looked at his wife, who was applying toenail polish.

"So how's the boy?" he said, finally breaking the silence. Sharon looked up from her toes. She knew to tread lightly.

"Good," she said. "He wakes me up every morning at 6:16 to the minute. I searched his room for an alarm clock since it's so precise. Other than that, he's terrific."

"Takes after his mother on that. For years, you woke at 7:06. Like clockwork."

"You noticed that?"

"One morning you stayed asleep until nine. I thought you were dead. So I nudged you," Lopez said.

"I remember that," she said, "Oh, to sleep til nine again. I would saw off an arm."

"You worry too much. Kale's three and you still fear crib death."

"I'm neurotic. It's part of why you married me," she said. Lopez neither agreed nor disagreed. "Last week I was at Pam's house and Kale was playing in the basement with some of the older kids," Sharon continued. "I left them alone for a few minutes to make drinks and I just got this bad feeling in my stomach. Pam's in the middle of this really heavy conversation about her mother's cervical cancer and I just run out of the room. She thought I was crazy.

"But I go downstairs and the two older kids have Kale under a blanket, sitting on him so he can't breathe. I pull up the blanket and he's purple and gasping for breath. He clings to me so tight, like he hasn't since he was an infant. Call me a helicopter parent, but I know my son and I know what he needs."

"I'm sorry you had to go through that alone," Lopez said. "Sorry I wasn't there."

Sharon pulled a long plastic pill case out of her purse and placed it on the floor. "This is for my anxiety," she said, pointing to a small blue pill. "This one's to sleep, this one's to wake up. These are Vitamin D."

"Don't you get Vitamin D from sunlight?" Lopez said.

"This is Celexa—I take a placebo dose. When I told the doctor I was taking five milligrams, he laughed. But look at this, Warren. I have to take all these just to make it through the day. This is who you married. I'm not an easy woman to live with. You knew that."

"I guess I did," said Lopez.

Sharon looked over at her husband and saw him grin.

"Remember when you used to give me half a Vicodin in exchange for watching *Twilight*?" Lopez said. "And the sequel was so bad I asked for the other half? The sex scene where the vampire's crying like, 'I wasn't gentle enough when we had sex.

Oh boo-hoo…'"

"You were in hell," said Sharon.

"You were in heaven."

"I have some, you know," she said.

Lopez scoffed. "Wait, I'm here with a gunshot wound and you've been hoarding vicodin?"

"You've been such a dick since I got here, you haven't deserved it," she said, tossing him three halves.

Twelve minutes later, Lopez lay with his head on Sharon's lap whistling *Blurred Lines*. Sharon gently stroked his balding head. "How'd we get this way, Sharon?" Lopez asked. "We used to have fun. Remember when we worked on that Elliot Smith documentary, and those yuppies were like, 'Who's Elliot Smith'? And we egged them?"

"You always bring that up when you're high," Sharon said.

"It was a classic. You were like, 'Explain that at the geezer home!' They were probably younger than we are now." Lopez laughed. "We really liked each other then, didn't we? We even worked well together as a team. All I ever wanted was to shoot documentaries, live in a little apartment in Los Feliz, and hang out with our friends. What happened?"

"You tried to get us things," Sharon said. "Nice things. Health insurance, the house, Kale."

"The years passed. And now this. My twenty-year-old self would hate me."

Sharon kissed her husband's forehead. Lopez felt a tear fall onto him.

"I wanted to tell you about the baby, Warren," Sharon said, her voice quavering. "I was just afraid."

"I knew it's what you wanted," Lopez said. "You left the signs everywhere."

"I'm sorry, Warren," Sharon sobbed.

"You have nothing to apologize for."

"I've been a miserable, horrible, demanding nag. You must hate me."

"You've been an amazing wife," said Lopez. "A real partner. You always gave me what I needed. And now you'll have what *you* need."

There was a pause as Sharon wiped her nose. "It's a girl," she said.

"Wow. I'm happy," Lopez said. "Did you tell Riffstein? I mean, he must be happy too."

"That jackass?" Sharon said. "Haven't seen him since. He moved to Connecticut for some new urology clinic. Half the reason I recruited him."

"Did you fall for him, Sharon? Just a little bit?" asked Lopez.

"Are you on crack?" Sharon said. "The guy's a slob. Dick's as small as an acorn. If the baby was a boy, I would have had it aborted to spare it from a life of disappointing women."

Lopez laughed until his foot throbbed. "Hey," Lopez said. "Let's do talk-talk."

"Talk-talk, now?" Sharon said.

"C'mon."

"Seriously, now?"

"Please?" Lopez said.

Sharon sighed, then looked up to the ceiling, thinking hard. "Okay, where to begin?" she said. "Okay, um, so I was thinking of getting blonde highlights in my hair..."

"I have to remember to Tivo the NBA finals," Lopez cut in.

"...Because my streaks are coming out and I'm starting to look like Katherine Beinstock," said Sharon.

"Spurs versus the Heat—not a great narrative, with two villains, but it's the beauty of the game, right?" Lopez said.

"...I wonder if Joanna can babysit if you're not back from work? Should only take two hours..."

"I wonder if Kale will watch the game with me? Eventually,

I'll teach him to play. The key is to dribble with both hands. Did I ever tell you that?"

"...She's outrageously expensive," Sharon said. "What teen-ager charges twenty dollars an hour for babysitting? I guess she's CPR certified..."

"He'll probably be tall," said Lopez. "Lots of people from the Ukraine are tall. You know I had a great uncle who was 6'6"?"

"...I should have been an interior designer," Sharon said.

Lopez burst out laughing, unable to continue, and gave his wife a high-five. Sharon laughed too, mostly out of relief. Their little joke about marital miscommunication never failed to connect them.

"I'm gonna get us out of here, babe," Lopez said, sitting up.

"You always get crazy ideas after we do talk-talk," said Sharon.

"I said, 'I'm gonna get us out of here.'"

"Warren, you're high. There's an armed terrorist outside the door. You've been shot once already. What are you going to do, teleport us?"

"Just hear me out," he said. His eyes shined. "We have to survive this. For Kale. For us. And for our little baby girl."

CHAPTER 6

It took some prodding to get the terrorists out of bed, and even after showers, they looked like death. Al-Asari was furious at his men's poor form, and as punishment made them wear their masks in the van even though the AC was busted.

TERRORIST #4 (INT.): "It was so hot that my balls were sweating balls... *what can this even mean??* " (*trimmed in post).

As for the cast of *Natural Dish-aster: Season Five,* they, like so many young chefs, had a superpower: the ability to recover quickly from a debilitating hangover using sunglasses and pills. It took them less than an hour to get into crisp chef whites and loaded into the van. T-Pain blasted out of their van's windows and everyone rapped along to the nasty bits.

Etienne sat in the back of the van next to LizZ. He unfolded a napkin to reveal two bird-shaped pastries that were flaky and buttery, topped with black sesame seeds. He handed one to LizZ. She took a bite and contemplated it for a moment, and Etienne bit into his. They searched each other's eyes for that glazed look they saw in fellow junkies right when the stuff hits the bloodstream.

"It's good. Really good," LizZ said. "But it's not..."

"It's not *it,*" Etienne sighed.

"We don't need to start over. It just needs..."

"Pistachios," said Etienne.

"Heavy cream," added Liz.

"Cardamom," said Etienne.

"Persimmon jelly."

Etienne grinned. "You are so bad..." He scribbled the additional ingredients on the napkin and tucked it away.

Across the van, Ghana eyed them suspiciously.

CHEF GHANA (INT.): "Now I know they're not having sex. That's for certain. But there's something fishy going on between those two, and I don't like it."

The drive along the Red Sea's hilly shoreline lasted well over an hour. Dirt roads led to rocky roads up windy hills with jagged cliffs. Waves crashed against the shore and booted eagles soared above, then dove down into the water for prey. The cast gazed out the window in utter wonder, but without the ability to remain silent even in the presence of jaw-dropping beauty—they continued to talk a hella o'shit.

"You know who was a bad ass chef?" Cowboy mused aloud. "The dude who cooked the Last Supper. That sonofabitch had some pressure. I mean, it's The Last Supper, right?"

"Imagine if Da Vinci's painting had Jesus staring down at some janky-ass chicken Caesar salad or like a molten lava cake, going, *really?*"

"Guy was Jewish. Probably sent food back to the kitchen all the time," said Etienne.

"You don't even pretend to not be anti-Semitic, do you?" Tanya said.

"When you think about it, Jesus was the first Jew for Jesus," said Cowboy. "I mean, he had to be."

"That's deep," said Ghana.

"Yunno, the thing about the Jews is...." Etienne began. / "Here we go again." / "What? I'm just saying that..." / "Someone make him stop." / "You have to admit that the Jews..." / "Are you like trying to start sentences that identify you as anti-

Semitic?" / "Just because I'm talking about Israel doesn't immediately mean…" / "You weren't talking about Israel—you were
talking about the Jews."

"Jesus Christ, would you guys shut the fuck up? I'm trying to
sleep," said Joaquim, who was way hung over. There were a few
seconds of respectful silence, and then…

"When you think about it, the first reality TV cooking competition challenge took place in Israel," said Cowboy.

"And it begins: the meanderings of an intellectual jackhole."

"All right, I'm up," said Joaquim, pissed. "Go ahead, genius,
tell us how the first reality TV cooking competition took place
in Israel."

"Simple," said Cowboy. "Everyone knows the Jews were slaves
in Egypt. Anyway, they escaped, and were running through the
desert for like forty years. But they didn't have time to bake
bread, seeing as they were being chased. So what do they come
up with?"

"Thrill us."

"Crackers," Cowboy said proudly.

"It's called matzah, Einstein," said Tanya.

"Right. So the challenge is, like, baking bread while running
through the desert almost getting murdered by slave owners."

"Can almost hear CJ Bazemore setting that up."

"I could go for some crackers right now," said Joaquim, "with
some red pepper hummus."

"Aw, it's so cute the way you mispronounce hummus," said
Clora. "It's hum, like hummer. You're phleming ch…"

"Choomoos," said Joaquim.

"Aww."

Cowboy was pissed. "Ask me, he's fucking illiterate."

"Screw you, Cowboy," said Joaquim.

"Fuck you, man, and your clown-ass ponytail."

"Oh, and that two-gallon hat isn't douchey at all…"

"I will hog-tie your ass in eight seconds flat."

"Take me only six seconds to carve you into a Thanksgiving turkey…"

"Children!" Clora broke in. "Can you please make peace for five seconds?" A beat.

"Fuck no!" they said in unison. And so the squabbling went on…

The terrorists' van followed close behind the cast's, but it was mostly quiet in there. Al-Asari had local radio on to make certain that the police were still unaware of his group's infiltration. As the van inched down a steep decline towards the shoot location, they passed several "off-limits" signs, including an old, faded billboard, written in several languages, warning of shark attacks in the area. One sign had dried blood on it.

"Where are they taking us?" one terrorist whispered nervously.

"Sshhaarrkkss," stuttered another. "Anything but sharks."

"It's breeding time, so they are particularly predatory," Sheik said. "And the water is warm, so that's even worse." The other terrorists shot him a look. Sheik shrugged. "What? I marathoned 'Great White Week' on The Shark Channel."

SHEIK (INT.): "Most people don't know that sharks have up to seven rows of replacement teeth. They go through thirty-thousand teeth in a life span, which isn't that surprising given that they've been known to eat boxes of nails for breakfast. Also, did you know that sharks can hear prey from over three-thousand miles away? Stop me if I'm boring you…"

The beach was located in a hidden cove, a sandy enclosure surrounded by ancient boulders. There were old rusty wires poking out of the ground, slabs of wood splayed out in odd places, rags and trash long abandoned in overturned buckets. It looked like something horrible had once happened there.

Cameras lined up in formation to cover a fifty-foot area

marked by pylons. Shovels leaned against two long cooking stations, each with built-in mini-stoves and a small, metal pantry. The cast and terrorists marched towards the beach and, staged in a semi-circle, were met by CJ Bazemore, who wore an understated gray-with-black-trim silk chef coat—the kind you might put on for a funeral.

"Well, well, well," Bazemore chided, looking at the party-ravaged faces. "Looks like someone's been sleeping with the enemy. Tsk-tsk!" Several of the female cast members grinned, while at least one terrorist bowed his head in shame.

Bazemore eyed his copy: "Welcome to Shalom-Risa Beach. During World War Two, when Jews faced extermination in Europe, merchants used this coast to smuggle refugees into Israel from Jordan. This small cove was a kind of Israeli Ellis Island, where over fourteen thousand Jews escaped annihilation. But one day, there was a shipwreck and, because these waters were heavily populated by sharks, most of the castaways did not survive."

Bazemore paused thoughtfully, before a grin spread across his face. "In today's *Cannibal Challenge*, you will walk in the shoes of those who escaped Hitler's clutches, and cook a dish native to his land... Apple strudel."

In the control room tent, Ruti threw up her hands. "Too stupid for words."

Sara shrugged. "Crisco integration. They wanted something with pie crust."

"Idiotic."

"Thematic."

"The twist," CJ Bazemore said, arching an eyebrow, "is that, to make your strudel, you'll start with only one ingredient—an apple. The rest of the ingredients, including more apples, are buried in coolers below the ground, and it's up to you to dig them out. Your time starts... now!"

Both teams ran to their shovels and commenced digging.

With only three shovels per team, the idea was that the other teammates would cheer the shovelers on. But that didn't rest well with the zealots of Team Mise En Bouche. While Etienne, Joaquim, and LizZ were shoveling big clumps of sand over their backs, the rest of the team got down and dug with their hands. In less than fifteen minutes, they had dug a coffin-sided hole, but no cooler was in sight.

CHEF CHRISSY (INT.): "The frustrating thing about this challenge is that you may dig a huge hole and find nothing, but the idea that, only inches away, you might find a cooler is too tantalizing to bear."

The terrorists dug hard too, and their good luck was almost immediate. After only twenty minutes, a great crack was heard and they pulled a red ice cooler out of the earth. It was packed with filo dough, bourbon, and sugar—essentially luxury items for a strudel.

Five coolers remained. Half an hour later, the terrorists found another cooler, this time containing cinnamon, raisins, and vegetable oil.

"*Ta Gueule!*" Chef Etienne said.

"You gots to be shitting me," said Cowboy.

Team Mise En Bouche passed the shovel to those without painful blisters. The rest continued to dig with their hands. An hour passed, then two and three. Half a dozen holes, all six feet deep and wide, and Mis En Bouche had nothing to show for their effort. The terrorists found a third cooler—salt, chocolate chips, and milk. Though they had almost enough to begin cooking, they kept on, wondering if they might find more apples or a substitute fruit.

Team Mis En Bouche hurled insults at the terrorists, calling them murderers and sluts. Another hour passed and the sun went down. People took naps. Chrissy lay on the sand and gazed up at the sky along with Ghana and Nisha, who pulled out a harmonica and played a basic blues riff.

A producer stepped in to remind Nisha to stick with public domain riffs because music clearance was an expensive nightmare. Nisha agreed. Ghana started to clap along to the harmonica; others joined in. "Well, I used to be a bigshot," Ghana sang, channeling Howlin' Wolf. "Used to drive in limousines."

"Preach!" called out Chrissy.

"Morgan Stanley cut my paychecks. How I loved that money green."

"Sing it, grrrl."

"But I quit it all for cooking, and for culinary fame. I sure wish someone warned me, I'd be unemployed and lame."

Ghana followed Nisha into the bridge. "So now I'm diggin' ditches..."

"She's digging ditches!" Joaquim shouted. "With aaaaaall my bitches!"

"That's right!"

"I got splinters on my hands, got sand in my teeth. I'm digging ditches..."

"With aaaaaaall her bitches!"

The cast hooted. Nisha hugged Ghana and they laughed so hard they fell onto each other in the sand. When they stopped laughing, their eyes met long enough for Chrissy to notice.

"Well, aren't you two a regular Burt Lancaster and Deborah Kerr?" she said.

"Who?" Nisha asked.

"*From Here to Eternity*?" Ghana said. "How old are you that you don't know that famous beach kiss?"

"Old enough to know that Burt and Deborah are names of two dead people, and dead people making out on a beach is gross."

"True that." Ghana patted sand off her pants. She helped Nisha up and they kept holding hands well after they were both standing.

In the pit, LizZ and Etienne shoveled side-by-side, whispering new ingredient combos that might work for their birdshaped pastry.

"Shallots," LizZ said, heaving sand over her shoulder, "with dried lavender flowers."

"Plum reduction," added Etienne, "and a pinch of black cocoa."

"Oh you are a naughty man," said LizZ.

At one point, Tanya found herself shoveling near the terrorists. Spotting Ramin, she noticed that his hands were raw, bleeding on the handle of his shovel. A strange maternal instinct sprang up inside her. "Here," Tanya said, and tossed a pink bandana at Ramin's feet.

The other terrorists just stared at her, but Ramin picked up the bandana and wrapped it around his hand. "I am deeply grateful," said Ramin, who continued to dig. Tanya wondered if she was going crazy by helping the terrorists win an important challenge.

Feeling tapped out, she let Cowboy dig in her place. Afterward, as Tanya watched Ramin dig, and saw him holding the bandana to his cheek and sniffing, she couldn't help but smile.

To everyone's surprise, local police showed up asking to see film permits, wondering just what in the hell was going on here. Sara took care of it. But when the cops called it in, the radio sequence was intercepted by a group of vacationing Israelis with a shortwave radio. They couldn't believe their ears when they heard that an American reality TV show was shooting at the infamously abandoned beach once known as Israel's Ellis Island. The vacationers decided to bring a party to the beach to watch. Soon, a police line was set up as dozens of drunkards and some environmental activists, watching to make sure none of the natural habitat was displaced, cheered on the diggers.

Al-Asari was pissed. "This was supposed to be low profile. One wrong move with the police and I give the order—everyone dies."

"Relax," said Sara. "They'll get bored and leave eventually."

The good thing about a challenge that forces cast members to engage in meaningless and frustrating activity is that drama is inevitable. Once Team Mise En Bouche tired of insulting the terrorists, they began to bicker among themselves. It was the usual cattiness expected from a reality cast. Even eye-rolls would play as story once they got interviews, but what Sara didn't expect was the discord among the terrorists. They spoke in Arabic, so Ruti became the *de facto* translator.

"They are saying that ISIS training camp in Syria was better than this. At least there was a point, killing infidels," she said. "And now, the four of them who did not go to ISIS training camp in Syria are claiming that the people who did train in Syria are always bringing that up whenever they can, like they went to Harvard or something, and they should shut up because right now they are all digging ditches."

"Wow, that is good stuff," Sara said.

"Just messing with you," said Ruti. "They're complaining about sand in their ass-cracks."

Chef Dex, aka Cowboy, began to dig a hole outside of the fifty-foot square. He did so feverishly, with the intensity of a man escaping prison. It was a burst of energy not seen in many hours. With each hurl of his shovel, he cried out. Tears streamed down his red and veiny face. One camera caught him close up and it appeared as though his eyes had rolled back in his head.

"Hey, genius, that's outside of the square," said Chef LizZ. "There's nothing over there."

"Cowboy, chill," Etienne implored him. "Save your energy, dude."

"He's trying to be a hero. Earth to Cowboy: You get more

camera time if you sleep with someone," said Joaquim.

"True that," said Tanya.

Cowboy, however, kept digging. His body was not under his control. He axed at the earth as if he was trapped and suffocating underground, with oxygen just on the other side. His shovel flew back and forth with such force that eventually the handle broke. But that didn't stop Cowboy. He got down on his knees and hacked away with the broken handle, desperate.

Some people in the crowd noticed and began to cheer him on, laughing and hurling insults in Hebrew. Cowboy dug more feverishly. He took the broken shovelhead and slammed it into the earth. His hands bled. Chef Ghana put a hand on Cowboy's shoulder and Cowboy bared his teeth and hissed.

"Devil's got him," Ghana said, backing off. "He's got exorcist eyes."

And then a crack. Unlike the sound made from the plastic coolers, it was more like the sound of bones breaking. In fact, the sound was so loud that the crowd promptly went silent, as did the crew.

Sara sat up in the control room and peered into the quad. "What happened?" she walkied her producers. "I said all coolers go in the square. Who fucked this up?"

"It's not a cooler," one of the Producers walkied back. "It must be something else."

"You sure?"

The jib camera stretched out above Cowboy.

"Did he make it to China?" a heckler yelled from the crowd, but the subdued laughter was mixed with curiosity.

Several of the chefs crowded around Cowboy. Tanya and Nisha got down on their hands and knees and dug along. Their hands met the edges of something hard, wooden. Their fingers explored the edges.

"What is it?" asked Chrissy.

"It's wood. Curved."

"Like the front of some old boat," said Nisha.

Cowboy rose to his feet as if he'd been yanked by strings. He threw his arms up to the heavens and again dropped to his knees. "Thank you, Lord!" he cried out. "For guiding my hand to your highness."

"What the hell is it?" Sara said.

Cowboy looked up to the jib camera. His eyes were insanely red, his face mapped by veins. A voice emanated from deep within him—a voice devoid of his trademark Texas twang, but low and guttural like Jabba the Hutt. "It's Noah's Ark," he said.

Then he fainted.

Tanya pulled out her iPhone and took a duckface selfie with the Ark framed in the background. "I'm totally going to win the internet!" she said, pushing her boobs together for another photo.

It was precisely at that moment that an impeccably manicured woman in a silk blouse and Jimmy Choo heels casually entered the control room tent, simultaneously texting on her Blackberry and sipping a chai tea latté.

"Is there anywhere in this country you can get decent Wi-Fi? I'm so behind on cuts," the woman said.

Sara recognized the voice of Genevieve Jennings, the Network Exec on *Natural Dish-aster: Season Five*, and said the only thing she could: "Oh shit."

"What is it?" Ruti asked.

Jennings looked up from her Blackberry, waved at Sara, rechecked her Blackberry, then made her way to Sara with the confident smile of someone used to getting good news from those she employed.

"Did I miss something?" she said.

"Genevieve, I was just going to call you," said Sara.

"Like hell you were, Sara. You've been dark for two days. Where's Lopez?" she said.

"He's sick. Bad hummus," said Sara.

"Lopez is never sick—I saw him eat a poisonous snake in Peru. He just added hot sauce. Didn't so much as burp. Where's Strider?"

"Ate the same hummus, I'm afraid. I'm looking over cameras," said Sara.

Jennings thought back to Sara's resumé and remembered something about her directing a couple of pilots for VH1. She wondered if they had any style, and decided that she would have to keep a close eye on the quad just in case.

"Any drama yet?" she asked, plunking down in the director's chair as if it had been waiting for her all along. "I want a full story download."

"Ms. Jennings, I presume," Al-Asari cut in, a charming smile spreading across his face. "Ms. Sinek didn't tell me what a natural beauty you are."

Jennings looked up at Al-Asari skeptically. She turned to Sara. "Who's this guy?"

"Our local consultant," said Sara. "To make sure everything's organic with the terrorists. He's highly respected in his community. Uniquely qualified."

"Yes, I'm the ISIS expert, and I've kidnapped your production! We will not relent until justice is done for The Network."

Jennings laughed, deciding to play along. She put up her hands. "What are your demands, you scary man?"

"Only the freedom of my people. But I would give all that up to have dinner with you tonight," Al-Asari said with a sly grin.

Jennings turned to Sara. "Is this guy serious?" she asked. When Sara nodded, Jennings blushed. "But I haven't even showered," she said, suddenly playing with her hair. "I'm all crunchy."

"We'll get you set up in a suite at the resort," Sara said.

"Great water pressure."

Jennings eyed Al-Asari and decided to make a dangerously un-PC joke. "Make sure the bed's extra sturdy too," she said.

Everyone erupted with laughter, including Al-Asari.

Nice call, Jennings, she said to herself.

On set, Team Mise En Bouche dug around the edges of the boat's enormous hull. Several bystanders broke through the police line to catch a glimpse of the biblical treasure. Tanya bent over to take another selfie. She stuck out her tongue, Miley-style.

"I'm going to call this one Noah's Twerk," she said, aiming her iPhone.

And that's when the police decided to shut down the shoot.

"Jesus Christ, Sara, this was supposed to be low profile," Genevieve Jennings said when they were in police custody.

"It was," said Sara.

"So you dig up proof of God's existence? That's your idea of low profile?"

"Cowboy went out of the zone. Some could call it a miracle," Sara said.

"Or a disaster. I'm not paying an overage on this if we have to postpone production. Won't do it. This one's on It-Is-What-It-Is."

An officious-looking man with a serious face and a small moustache entered the room and sat across from the two women. "Guard, some water for our guests," he instructed the tall man with a uni-brow who stood at the door. As water was poured into plastic cups, the officer eyed Sara and Jennings. Then he frowned. "We checked your papers," he said. "Every-thing is in order."

"Well, that's a relief," said Sara.

"However, we have a problem with your statement," the officer said.

"But it's just like we went over," said Sara. "One of our chefs dug outside of the marked area and…"

"Yes, Chef Dex McNaughton, or 'Cowboy' as you call him," the officer said. "Tell me, what is Cowboy's background?"

"Uh, he's from Texas," Sara said.

"Yes, yes. Not too big of a Jewish population in Texas, is there?"

"Not too sure what that has to do…"

"Quite small for America, actually. In fact, I noticed that there are very few Jews in your entire cast. Why is that?" asked the officer.

"We didn't realize it would be an issue," said Jennings.

"Not an issue, just an odd choice. But Chef Tanya. Yes, Chef Tanya Lazar. Not only is she Jewish but Bat Mitzvahed in Tel Aviv, right here in Israel. Isn't that amazing?"

"I suppose it is."

"Oh, it is," the officer smiled. "And so isn't it absolutely remarkable that a Jewish girl who was Bat Mitzvahed right here in the land of her forefathers would be the one to discover…"

"But she didn't…"

"What a story!" marveled the officer. "That Tanya Lazar, the sole Jew in your cast, a real beauty too, would be led by God to reveal a treasure of our past. And your little television show goes on without pause. But with Chef Cowboy from Texas discovering it, there might be problems. Permits misplaced, fines for ripping up the beaches, footage seized for investigation…"

"Is he suggesting an overage?" Jennings said to Sara, nervously. "Because we can't have one."

"We understand completely," said Sara. "It was Tanya who discovered Noah's Ark. That is, as you said, absolutely remarkable."

"Did you just say Noah's Ark?" the officer said, having burst out laughing. "Ha ha! You secular Jews and your biblical fantasies! Noah's Ark? Now that's rich! Raffi, did you hear that?" The uni-brow at the door chuckled. "Someone here has a touch of Jerusalem Syndrome, no?" the officer said. "No, no. What was found by none other than Tanya Lazar was part of a ship that brought Jewish refugees through the Red Sea during the Holocaust. We thought the boat was lost at sea, with everyone devoured by sharks. But miraculously, it was right there on the beach. Noah's Ark. Ha! You people!"

The officer laughed heartily. He looked at Sara. Sara laughed. Sara looked at Jennings. Jennings laughed. The guard with the uni-brow joined in again, laughing too. "So, we are clear about who made the discovery?" said the officer.

"Like a summer's day," Sara replied.

"Excellent," the officer said. "Tanya is an amazing patriot to the Israeli people. A true member of the tribe."

Just then a bald bespectacled man with a clipboard appeared at the door. "Ah, here's the reporter from The Times," the officer said. "Let him know exactly what happened today. Everything you told me. Hold nothing back."

"Copy that," said Sara.

"Madame," the officer said to Jennings. He bowed and kissed her hand softly before walking out.

Jennings turned to Sara, blushing. "What is it about these Middle Eastern men? Am I really that bang-able here?"

After Sara and Jennings were released from the Eilat Police headquarters, they discovered Tanya surrounded by a frenzy of reporters outside.

"I just felt this divine light," Tanya said into the throng of microphones. "It was Hashem urging me to reconnect with my ancestors."

"Will you make Alliyah, Tanya?" a reporter asked.

"Totally!" she said. "Hey, do you guys want to hear my Torah portion? I think I still totally remember it. Vay-itaaaain, Et-Ha Shulraaaaan veyole helmo-ed...."

Sara grabbed Tanya's elbow and led her away from the crowd. "Enough for now. Thanks!" Sara told the press.

There was an audible sigh from the crowd of delighted reporters. Tanya blew them kisses as she was hustled off into a van.

"Oh my Gawd," she tittered. "I'm gonna get so many new Instagram followers, it's sick."

CHAPTER 7

Genevieve Jennings' rigorous pre-date beauty regimen included an Ahava Dead Sea mud-mask facial followed by an hour-long soak in fragrant sea salts while surrounded by lavender aromatherapy candles. She did this all while typing out fourteen pages of notes on a Fine Cut 3 version of a half-hour pilot about chef tattoos. "More tattoo porn!" was a recurring note, along with "music needs an overall re-think."

She tried on three outfits, six pairs of heels, and seven different jewelry combos before dousing her wrists with a perfume endorsed by Rihanna.

Genevieve Jennings was in total control of every aspect of her life—from how she looked (think Kerry Washington at the Emmys), to her brilliant rising career as a television executive, to the way she categorized her friends and family. She was the envy of her high school reunion; the woman who had it all. Everything except for the obvious. She had never figured out men.

Sure, she could produce a hit series about the psyche of men in the online dating world (winning two Digital Emmy Awards, thank you very much). But face to face with their hungry eyes, thoughtless grooming, and constant advances and retractions, men made Genevieve Jennings feel completely out of control. So much so that when Al-Asari knocked on her hotel room door, Jennings flinched, spilling her three-hundred dollar Rihanna fragrance all over the floor. "Fuck," she said, sopping it up with a towel. "Fuck. Fuck. Fuck." She tossed the towel into the closet and kicked it shut. Al-Asari knocked again. "A minute!" Jennings called out. She peered into the mirror. "You can do this, Jennings. Go out there and be amazing. Master of your domain... master of your domain." She took a deep breath, exhaled slowly, then opened the door.

Al-Asari held out a bouquet of roses. "You look ravishing," he said.

Jennings froze. *Say something.* "White roses," she blurted. "My favorite color!" Then she thought, *Wait, is white even a color anymore or more of a shade? Kind of the way Pluto was downgraded from a planet to a big ball of ice? Who keeps up on astrology anyway?*

"Do you mean astronomy?" Al-Asari said.

"What?"

"You said astrology. I think you might mean astronomy. The study of planets," Al-Asari said.

It was then that Jennings realized she'd been speaking her thoughts aloud.

"Yes! Astronomy! Ha, what a dummy," she said. "I actually produced a series on the planets for PBS when I first got started. Samuel L. Jackson was supposed to voice it, but we ended up with Blair Underwood instead, so you know, kaput ratings. Did you watch *LA Law?*"

"I don't think so," said Al-Asari.

"Of course not. Why would you? My senior year at Sarah Lawrence, I had my deviated septum operated on and I watched the whole series before binging was even a thing."

"How interesting."

"Well, depends who you ask," said Jennings. She smiled. This was okay. She was happy just to be talking. *That had to be better than awkward silence, right?*

"Shall we?" said Al-Asari, extending his arm.

"What happened to your hand?" Jennings said, noticing the

bandage there.

"Oh, an old lady next door locked herself out of her house. When I climbed onto the roof to go in through her attic, my hand caught on a shingle."

"Oh, you poor thing."

"As it turned out, she had the keys in her purse the whole time," said Al-Asari. "My fault for not asking."

Jennings smiled. Her eyes sparkled. "Well, let's go." And just like that, Louboutin heels clicked down the hall and Jennings entered a taxicab alongside her date, a man she'd met on set, a handsome-if-professorial-looking man from the Middle East. *So what about it?*

They cabbed it down-beach to a nearby hotel restaurant. It was dimly lit with white tablecloths and red bouquets at each table.

"This is the kind of place where people propose," Jennings chuckled. "Did you bring the ring? Heh, heh."

"Table for two?" asked the maître d'.

"Unless you'll be joining us," Jennings said, unable to stop herself.

"Right this way," the maître d' said.

Al-Asari pulled out a chair for Jennings, then sat and folded a napkin across his lap. Jennings also folded her napkin across her lap, but then couldn't think of what to do with her hands. She felt them flap around like fish on the table. She checked if the salt and pepper caps were properly tightened. They were. And even though countless therapy sessions had been spent analyzing why she had the habit of flapping her hands around when she was nervous, she just couldn't stop.

"Dating scares the hell out of me," she admitted finally. "There, I said it. I blather—I'm blathering now. And my hands flap. I date online too because where do you meet people these days? But it never works. Not one good date. Well, one, but... oh forget it. Have I got stories…"

"I understand," said Al-Asari.

"You do?" she said, surprised. "I think I'd remember your Match profile."

"Oh, I didn't mean…"

"I think I was one of the first online daters," said Jennings. "I mean since MySpace. I recently tried Tinder, but the idea of people swiping me away with their finger—well, that creates a whole new business of creating the perfect profile pic. Do you know there are consultants now who help you develop your online persona? Even help you take selfies so you don't look too, well, selfie-conscious. Ha, talk about a scam."

"Why would you want to claim to be someone you are not?" asked Al-Asari.

"Oh, I don't know. Marketing?" Jennings laughed too loudly. She looked at her empty wine glass. "Wow, who do I have to blow around here to get a Chardonnay? I mean, does the waiter have any next of kin?"

"Genevieve?" Al-Asari said.

"I'm burning up…"

"Genevieve."

"Yes?"

"We are simply two adults sitting down for a meal," Al-Asari said. "You are an attractive and accomplished woman. I am an interested man who wishes to get to know you. It is that simple. There's no need to be anxious. You don't even have to consider this a date if that makes you feel more comfortable."

"Of course. I understand," she said, hands flapping away.

"So, as two adults simply sitting down to dinner, tell me about yourself. What do you really love in life, Genevieve Jennings?"

"Me? Oh well. What a question!" Jennings said. "I'm, uh, I'm really into my career, obviously. And, uh, finding solutions to the new challenge of transmedia storytelling. That's the new frontier. People will all be watching TV on their iWatches in a minute, don't you think?"

"I suppose so."

"Well, they will. Research proves it. So the key is finding a way to tell stories that seamlessly flow from on-air entertainment to digital without breaking story. It all has to be additive. Am I speaking too fast?"

"Just fine."

"Oh, I don't know. Work has really been stacking up, and of course this is a very important show for me. Glen says my promotion depends on it. I could run Non-Scripted if this one hits. Of course he's been dangling that carrot in front of my nose for years. I think it's a big power game. Do you know that he didn't invite me to his birthday party? Claims his assistant messed up the Evite. Then why not fire her? I hate that smug Berkeley bitch."

The waiter arrived and Jennings ordered two chardonnays with ice cubes and then asked what Al-Asari wanted.

"Sparkling water," he said.

"Listen to me blathering on," said Jennings. "You! When you aren't a terrorist consultant for TV shows, what do you do with your free time?"

"I have a dog," Al-Asari replied.

"Interesting."

"She is what you Americans call a therapy dog, but she is not trained. I found her amidst the rubble of a war in my home village. She is gifted with sick people. Born to bring them happiness. So on weekends, I take her to hospitals and to the bedsides of the terminally ill. It's the least I can do. It's amazing what a little touching can do."

"Yes, very therapeutic."

"Give me your hands," Al-Asari said.

"Excuse me?"

Al-Asari reached across the table and placed Genevieve's hands in his own. He rubbed his thumbs along her palm, kneading the tension from the center to the outer edges. "As humans, we yearn to be touched and yet, here we sit, feet away from each other," he said. "Across tables, afraid to be the first to make contact. Afraid of being misunderstood. In my culture, we always hold hands. It lowers stress. In my community, there is surprisingly little heart disease—and this despite an illegal foreign occupation. Because we touch. Isn't that remarkable?" He slowly moved his hands to her wrist. She closed her eyes. "Tell me—how does that feel?"

"It's, um, nice," Jennings said. Her face flushed.

"And?"

"Um, I feel relaxed. Almost peaceful."

"Exactly. Human touch—it is the least prescribed medicine in the Western World. Where I am from, it is primary medicine."

Jennings' hands closed onto Al-Asari's. Her fingernails dug into the bandage on his left hand. "I feel it. I'm really feeling it," she said.

"Yes. Let your hands explore... That's good."

"Yes." Jennings let out a little moan. "Yes, I really feel it..."

"*More wine?*" the waiter cut in.

"Wha—?" Jennings crashed back to earth, her eyes popped open, and she pulled her hands away from Al-Asari's. "Yes, um... No. Later! Okay, one more pour." She took a long swig, then pointed back at the glass for a topper.

"Sorry," she said to Al-Asari. "Seems I lost myself for a moment."

"That's good," said Al-Asari. "We all need that."

"You're an interesting man, Mr. Al-Asari," Jennings said, taking another gulp of wine.

"Call me Izzeldin," he said.

"Exotic," Jennings said. "So tell me, Izzeldin, how did you move into this line of work?"

"Let us not talk of work," Al-Asari said. "Let us discuss pleasure. Outside of work, what brings you the most pleasure, Genevieve?"

Jennings thought about it. She moved close as if to reveal a secret that might get a little naughty. "Honestly?" she said. "Sit-down interviews."

"Interviews."

"When I was a segment producer on *Today*, I used to love doing sit-down interviews. Getting to the bottom of stories, calling people out on their bullshit while they're in the chair, making them cry. Oh, I had a talent for criers. When I was at Media Nine, I tallied the most cries in company history. Won a Kindle Fire. Then I moved to the Network side and it's just notes, notes, and more notes. I never get to be back in that interviewer's chair."

"If that is what you love, then you must do it," said Al-Asari.

"I know, I know. But how?"

"I believe you will find a way, Genevieve Jennings." Al-Asari raised his sparkling water. "To you, and to sit-down interviews."

Jennings raised her glass and smiled. There was a glint in her eyes. She was really connecting with this guy.

CHAPTER 8

The next day, in the calm, marble-laden cast mansion overlooking the Gulf of Aqaba, the cast of *Natural Dishaster: Season Five* sat in a circle engrossed in their Elimination Deliberation. They were separated from the terrorists, who had their own deliberation taking place on the upper veranda.

"I say Tanya gets immunity," said Chef Chrissy, strategically. "She knows the culture here, and that could really help if challenges start to get more Jew-y."

"I once dated an orthodox rabbi," Chef LizZ reminded the group. "Plus, Tanya admitted that she's never even heard of Kabbalah."

"All in favor of Tanya's immunity?" said Chrissy. Seven chefs raised their hands. Tanya blew them kisses.

"Horseshit," LizZ said.

"I say Cowboy goes into the elimination battle," said Chef Joaquim. "He totally went off the reservation with his digging, and how did that help us?"

"He found Noah's Ark," said Etienne. "Do you realize how world altering that shit is? He's giving hope to Bible freaks everywhere."

A field producer stepped in to remind the group that, per their earlier conversation, it was Tanya who had found Noah's Ark, not Cowboy. And it wasn't Noah's Ark anyway. It was a lost boat for European Jewish refugees.

"Sorry, forgot," said Etienne.

"Joaquim should go," said Cowboy. "He's always complaining, and that negativity really affects the team during cooking."

"Bullshit," said Joaquim. "And you know what? This is stupid! Why do we have to sit around a fireplace, anyway? So fucking *Survivor.*"

"What'd I tell ya?" said Cowboy.

"Why shouldn't you cook in the elimination, Joaquim?" Chef Ghana asked.

"Because fuck you," said Joaquim.

"Watch your mouth," said Nisha, and Ghana appreciated that.

"I agree with Cowboy," said Tanya.

"The problem is Joaquim knows all the Spanish dishes," said Clora. "What if they spring like a Sephardic Molé on us? He's all we've got."

Cowboy didn't like Clora defending Joaquim, and he hated how happy Joaquim seemed that she did.

"I trained in Spain," Chef Nisha said. "I can handle it."

"You externed for like a week at a tapas joint on Las Ramblas," Clora said.

"It was intense. I learned a lot."

"You know what?" Cowboy said, seeing an opportunity to impress Clora. "I'll do it. If Joaquim's too chicken-shit, then a real man has to step in."

"No, Cowboy," Clora protested. "You're one of the team's most important chefs. No one does barbeque like you."

Cowboy smiled. "Well, thank you, baby. But I'm confident in who I am as a chef. I can beat whoever they put in front of me, so keep the bed warm for me, doll. It's settled."

"All in favor?"

"Thank you," Clora whispered to Cowboy. She touched his

hand. But seconds later, Clora stole a glance at Chef Joaquim, who grinned and winked at her conspiratorially. Unfortunately, Cowboy saw. "I've changed my mind," Cowboy said. "I'm not going anywhere."

"But you just said it's settled," said Joaquim. "That's some Indian giving."

"Let's not get racist," said Cowboy. "Besides, cowboys can't be Indians. That's just foolishness."

In the control room, Al-Asari scoffed. "How can television be made of this?"

"This is the gold," said Sara. "Blatant self-preservation under the veil of dignity. Relatable, wouldn't you say?"

Ruti flipped audio channels to hear the terrorists' deliberations on the upper veranda. Per Genevieve Jennings' request, Sara had prepped the terrorists to display "the culture of martyrdom so popular with Islamic fundamentalists." So, unlike Team Mise En Bouche, the men of Mal-Malaika fought over who would have the honor of competing in the elimination round.

"I was by far the strongest digger, so I must go to the elimination round," Sheik said.

"But I found the cooler with the filo dough. So it must be me that goes," said Mohammed.

"You slacked after that. I saw you napping. So you must be safe from elimination," said Tarik.

"I should go," said Farkha. "I can feel that it is my turn... I have spoken to Allah*" (*additional audio added in post).

"I have such a feeling as well" (*additional audio added in post).

"Me too" (*additional audio added in post).

"Well, one thing's for sure, Azeem should not go. He was terrible at digging, and what's more, he pissed himself in bed last night."

"You promised not to tell!" said Azeem.

"I only said I would not tell right away," said Tarik.

"Son of a goat!" (*additional audio added in post).

In the control room, Jennings licked her chops at all the organic drama. Since last night's date with Al-Asari, she'd felt shy when around him, hoping to impress him with her authority on set, but careful not to be too bitchy. When the 2nd AD read out the production schedule, explaining that sit-down interviews were scheduled to occur right after deliberations ended, Al-Asari glanced at Jennings with an expectant look on his face, and she went for the bait.

"Who's doing sit-downs?" she asked, casually.

"I am," an experienced producer named Amanda Winter said.

"You'll make them cry, right?" asked Jennings.

"Absolutely," said Amanda.

"How?" Jennings asked.

"Excuse me?"

"How will you make them cry? What's your closer? You do have a closer, right?"

The Producer thought about it. "I'll ask them how it made them feel when the others tried to vote them into the elimination," she said.

Jennings scoffed. "No, no, no! God, don't they teach producers this stuff anymore?" she said. "Okay, I'm going to share with you the fail-safe rule for making a cast member cry. If they have kids, ask them if they miss their kids. If they don't have kids, ask them if they think their parents are proud of them. That's the simple rule for making people cry in interview."

Jennings winked at Al-Asari, who looked impressed. Amanda Winter scribbled in her notepad. "Okay got it... 'Do you think that your parents are proud of...'"

"You know what? I'll do the interviews," Jennings said. "I may be a bit rusty, but I still have some gas in the tank. I produced two seasons of *Celebrity Pre-nup Challenge*." Jennings stared intently at Amanda, expecting her to be awestruck.

Instead, Amanda shot Sara a look that asked, "Is this shit really happening?"

"That's a great idea," Sara said to Jennings, "But we really need you in the control room for story support."

"Don't try to talk me out of it, Sara," Jennings cut in. "I can have you replaced in a snap."

Sara looked at Amanda and shrugged. *What can I do?*

Jennings beamed at Al-Asari. She hadn't felt this in control in a while.

Lighting took their time with green screen tweaks while Jennings, cigarette in hand, paced the hall outside the interview room.

"Ah, to smoke indoors again. I love Israel," she said.

Sara had placed Tanya at the top of the interview list because she'd surely give Jennings the required waterworks. Tanya never left an interview dry-eyed, however crocodile the tears might be, and Jennings sure wouldn't know the difference. The room was small and intimate, perfect for an emotional one-on-one.

The Cast Wrangler led Tanya down the hall, placed her in the interview chair, and had her given a touch-up of powder. She looked like a wreck, primed for a major emotional breakdown.

Jennings entered the room like a champion boxer into the ring—cocksure and strutting. She took a seat left of camera, across from Tanya, and smiled unctuously.

"Hello, Tanya," Jennings said. "I'll be doing your interview today."

"Loving that," Tanya smiled.

"Great, because I want to go deep, okay?" said Jennings.

"Really get into your feelings. Let's you and me agree to skip the bullshit and get right to the authentic stuff. Deal?"

"I like that," said Tanya. "Let's get raw."

Jennings grinned. *This is going to be a cinch.* "Wonderful, because you've been through a hell of a lot lately: Brandon's fall and kidnapping, the terrorist infiltration, your discovery of an ancient Jewish artifact. Let's start with Brandon. I know you two had a deep connection."

Tanya's eyes were already wet. "We did."

"And so it must have been hard for you to see him hurt. Describe for me, Tanya, what's it like to see someone you care for so deeply now in such great pain?"

Tanya thought back to Brandon's fall, but the image that kept pushing its way into the front of her brain was Ramin, that pencil-necked terrorist poet kid, sweetly caressing her pink bandana at the beach dig. She couldn't go there, so she blurted: "Brandon's a tough cookie. I'm sure he'll be fine."

Tanya looked at Jennings to confirm she'd nailed it, but Jennings frowned.

"Need another take?" asked Tanya, experienced in reading the reactions of producers.

"No, that was cool," Jennings said, forcing a smile. She scribbled a note on her clipboard. "Just looking for a bit more emotion. I mean, don't you feel the slightest bit guilty?"

"Why?"

"Well, you were the one distracting him with the megaphone. You don't think maybe it contributed to his injuries?"

"There's a famous rugby saying in South Africa," Tanya said. "'Don't hate ze playa, hate ze game.' So, yeah."

"Interesting," said Jennings, knowing an opportunity to switch gears when she saw it. "You grew up in South Africa, right, hence your knowledge of the local vernacular. I'm curious as to what that was that like, I mean given the political and racial tensions in that region."

"I was born after Apartheid," said Tanya. "Mandela was President when I was like three. I remember him meeting with the Spice Girls. So that was pretty cool."

"Cool. Huh," said Jennings. "But your parents are still there? Part of the white minority?"

"They moved to Rhode Island ages ago."

"Tanya," Jennings said, her eyes flashing. "Tanya, do you think that your parents are proud of you?"

When Tanya's face went pale, Jennings almost chuckled. *Works every time. Turn on the faucet, baby. Rookies can't handle this shit.*

"My parents?" Tanya said, lower lip quivering. "I guess I don't really care what my parents think."

"Why's that?"

"Well, because they kind of stole all my money from Season One. You know that I can't really talk about that, legally, right? That was a big Network thing."

"Yes, I know," said Jennings. "It's just that it must be hard for you, having your parents betray you like that. How did that make you feel?"

"It sucked," Tanya said, face tightening. She turned to the audio guy. "Didn't I already cover this in pre-interview? I mean, I discovered Noah's Ark, and I'm being asked how I feel about my parents?"

"I just want to understand how you feel," Jennings said.

"You wanna know how I feel?" Tanya reached for her lav mic and yanked it out. "I feel like I just got my period." Tanya stood up, turning to Audio. "Can you de-mic me? Thanks, Dougie."

Jennings sat there stunned as the audio guy removed Tanya's mic. "What in the hell are you doing?"

"Women issues are an automatic pass," said Dougie. "Network policy."

"I know that!" Jennings snapped.

"That was lots of fun. Bye, Felica," Tanya said, bounding out of the room.

Jennings snarled when she noticed that Tanya was wearing white pants. *No way that chick's on the rag.*

"She must be in shock from everything that happened," Sara said, stepping in to assure Jennings. "Let's bring in the next guy. Here's his story one-sheet. Checkmarks next to the topics we've already covered."

"I don't need that!" Jennings sneered at the paper as if it was coated in feces. "This is about emotion, not checkmarks. See, that's the problem with producers today."

Jennings took a long hit of Diet Coke as Chef Dex, aka Cowboy, sat down in the interview chair. Jennings waved Sara off, then smiled coolly at Cowboy as he was mic'd up.

"Dex," Jennings said once camera was speeding, "you volunteered to go into the elimination round, but your team didn't exactly fall over themselves to stop you. How did that make you feel?"

"Bad," Cowboy said.

"Good," Jennings grinned. "Can you elaborate a bit?"

"Real bad?" said Cowboy. "As in, pissed off."

"Fantastic," said Jennings. "And it must have been doubly painful when you saw Clora look over to Joaquim and smile when you volunteered to go in."

"It was," said Cowboy, his cheeks getting red.

"Pretty obnoxious, actually," Jennings scoffed. "I mean to be so brazen in front of you. You clearly have feelings for Clora, and there she is, practically flaunting the fact that she's been secretly hooking up with Joaquim."

"She what?!" Cowboy's face contorted in confusion and rage. "Son of a bitch! I'll kill him. I'll string him up!" Cowboy ripped off his mic and stomped out of the room, irate. Jennings cringed.

She had broken reality TV's only rule: Never reveal story to your subjects. And now, in the middle of interview, Cowboy was off to chase down Joaquim and beat his ass. To follow that action, Sara repo'd a camera crew then on meal break. They were sizzling pissed to have to get up.

The next interview went just as badly. When Jennings asked Chef Ghana if she missed her kids, a long convoluted story came out about how the producers secretly let her Facetime with them, so she didn't really miss them much at all. When a PA peeked in to take coffee orders, Jennings yelled at him for breaking her flow, then added: "Yes, a triple caramel latté." She mumbled to herself, "Little shit implying I don't have the juice to handle some interviews?"

She turned to Sara. "This cast is full of duds. Like getting blood from a stone. Bring in one of the terrorists," she said.

Sara hesitated. "Not sure if that's such a good idea."

"Now!" Jennings said.

One of the masked terrorists, Farkha, was herded into the interview room and mic'd up.

He sat across from Genevieve Jennings in his black ski mask and red kafyiah, his AK-47 machine gun leaning at his side so the tip could be seen in frame.

"I'm going to ask you a few questions," Jennings said to the terrorist. "And I don't want you to answer right away. I want you to explore your feelings on the matter. Don't be afraid to really get in touch with your feelings. Understand?"

The terrorist nodded.

"Good. So, how does it feel to be face to face with a woman with power right now? A woman with her face uncovered, educated, free from man's oppression?"

"It feels neither good nor bad," Farkha said.

"Oh, that's interesting," said Jennings. "And what if I told you that I've had three abortions? Would that upset you?"

"I would feel bad that you went through that, I suppose," he said, sheepishly. His body took on a defensive posture.

"Oh, okay, right," said Jennings. "And then tell me—and take your time answering this—how does it feel to be a fucking murderer of innocent women and children?!"

"Let's take a short break," Sara said, stepping in. "Audio issue."

Jennings paced the hall, waving a cigarette. "I know what you're going to say, Sara, but I want him angry. I want that real emotion. If this is going to work, all I can be to him is a piece of American meat—an infidel. Let's explore his real feelings on the matter."

"Absolutely," Sara said. "And we will. But we usually wait until we get the basic story info out of them first. So we don't have to do pick-ups, which might get costly."

Jennings understood the subtext about overages. "Good plan," she said.

Stubbing out her cigarette, Jennings walked back in. The terrorist repositioned himself in his chair, clearly uncomfortable with her presence.

"Sorry about that," Jennings smiled. "I'm guilty of getting a bit too into story sometimes. We all get too into our jobs at some point, right?"

"I am sure that your position is stressful," the terrorist said.

"And what stresses you out?" Jennings asked, coolly. *A good solid question.*

"Well, I suppose that I..."

Suddenly, Jennings lunged out of her chair and grabbed the terrorist's machine gun. She planted her feet wide apart and pointed the barrel directly in his face. "Not one move or everyone gets wet!" Jennings yelled. The terrorist reeled back, shielding his face between his fingers. Sara put her hands up along with everyone else in the room.

"Pplleeaassee don't shoot!" the terrorist said. He shook in

his flimsy chair.

"Feeling pretty powerless, huh?" asked Jennings. "Now that I've got the gun?"

"Y-yes, that's exactly how I feel," the terrorist stuttered.

"Does this mean you're ready to drop the attitude? To give me the emotion I need?"

"Anything!" the terrorist cried.

"Tell me, do you have any kids?" asked Jennings.

"Nephews," he replied.

"Oh yeah? You miss 'em?"

"Excuse me?" the terrorist asked.

"Do. You. Miss. Them?" Jennings said.

"Well... yes, of course."

"I don't believe you," said Jennings. Her voice was like that of a drill sergeant. "How much do you miss them? Make me understand."

"I miss them a lot," he said.

"Cry for them."

"Excuse me?"

"Cry. For. Them."

The terrorist's eyes widened. He scrunched up his face. "Booooo-hooo!" he said. "Oh boo-hoo!"

"I don't buy it," said Jennings, rolling her eyes. "I need to believe you!"

"Booo-hoooo-hoooo!"

"Now!" a PA yelled.

Audio jumped onto Jennings' back, the PA went for her feet, and the camera op grabbed the gun. Jennings bit down hard on the camera op's hand and got loose long enough to point the gun in the general direction of the terrorist and drag her finger back onto the trigger. The gun sprayed in every direction. The terrorist flew back in his chair and hit the ground. Round after round shot out until only clicks of an empty barrel could be heard.

"She's secure!" said Audio.

Jennings flailed but the crew wrestled her onto her back. "You sons of bitches! I'll have you all fired for this!" she screamed. "I'm Vice President of Current Programming at The Network. Do you have any idea what I can do to your careers? You'll never work again!"

That's when the audio guy went too far. He pulled back and clocked Jennings in the nose. Her eyes went cross, a small trickle of blood came out of one nostril, and everything went black. **AUDIO GUY (INT.):** "I live by two simple rules: I show up for work on time, and I don't respond well to threats. Apparently, Miss Fancy Pants Vice President didn't get the memo."

Sara and Al-Asari stood out on the balcony trying to make sense of the fact that Genevieve Jennings, the Network's VP of Current Production, was hog-tied on the floor of the laundry room, a ticking time bomb for the whole crew.

"Interesting day," Al-Asari said.

"Day ain't over yet," Sara said.

"This is not insurmountable," said Al-Asari. "It mustn't be."

"Kidnapping a Network Exec? No, you're right. That's nothing."

"At least no one got hurt," Al-Asari said. "A miracle really."

"You think so? Because to me, it's a huge problem," said Sara.

"I don't follow," said Al-Asari.

Sara lit a cigarette. "Jennings sprayed a full clip in there."

"Yes."

"Well, no one got so much as a scratch," said Sara.

"Like I said, a miracle."

"Or the gun had blanks," Sara said. "Which makes me wonder if you guys have any bullets at all. I'm pretty certain that's what the crew's thinking."

"Oh, we have bullets alright," said Al-Asari.

"The crew probably thinks this is all bullshit. Probably all scheming to revolt right now."

"We shot Lopez," said Al-Asari.

"Yes, you did shoot Lopez," Sara said.

"If you suspect us of being unarmed, a better question might be why you haven't turned on us already?" said Al-Asari. "You've had several opportunities. Why not?" Sara didn't answer. Al-Asari smiled. "I'm sure you have your reasons," he said. "Want to know what I think motivates you?"

"Thrill me," said Sara.

"You know that we're not terrorists. That we had nothing to do with the bombing in Haifa."

"Oh, that's real plausible. You're all over the news escaping in vans…"

"Do you know what Mal-Malaika means in Arabic?" asked Al-Asari. "It means 'with the angels.' Each one of us in our group has had a friend or family member killed in this war with Israel. I visited America once—Albuquerque—and a good friend was in a support group for people who'd lost loved ones—a survivor's group. It helped him.

"So when I came back to the West Bank, I started such a support group. Only a few of us came at first. We talked. Some talked of revenge—some had gotten themselves involved in bad things. But it was a place to talk. To heal. The authorities had us on some list. I went in to speak to them about it. I tried to explain that we were non-violent.

"They detained me. Three weeks on a dirt floor, no lawyer, no phone calls. A piss-stained bag on my head for hours a day.

They had me chained to a radiator and made me sit in awkward positions until my back burned. Once, I blacked out from the pain."

"If you think I have some kind of sympathy for you..."

"After I got out of jail, I found that the group had split off," said Al-Asari. "And they were making all kinds of plans for revenge. I tried to talk them out of it—to say that violence would lead to nothing. But then we were raided. The Israelis had discovered the plans. And there was a shoot-out. Did people die? I don't know, but I wish to God, no.

"My instinct was to pay penance, but after what I had experienced in jail, after the cruelty I had experienced despite being innocent, I fled. We packed up and came here. If ever we needed to flee, Ruti's father once told us, we could be safe on these grounds in Eilat. He said it was hidden in plain sight," he said. "Oh, but how this place has changed. And we certainly didn't expect you to be here."

Al-Asari looked at Sara. "We are broken men, Ms. Sinek— alone with our pain, our dreaded memories, the emptiness left by the friends and families who have died in this mess. That is our motivation—to start over. Tell me, what motivates you, Ms. Sinek. Is it your esteemed career? Your family?"

"Money," Sara said. She stubbed out her cigarette. "I need money."

"For your brother?"

"Doesn't matter," Sara said. Looking around to see if anyone was in earshot, she lowered her voice. "I have a plan, okay? If it works, I can get you and your men out of here, with some cash for a fresh start. And I'll get what I want," she said. "But you'll have to follow my lead."

"I'm listening."

"Question first," said Sara.

"You get only one," said Al-Asari.

"How are you at scuba?"

Outside Jennings' makeshift cell, Ruti briefed Sara and Al-Asari on the disaster within. "She chewed through the duct tape," Ruti said. "She's like a wild animal or something."

Sara arched an eyebrow to Al-Asari. "You ready?"

"Now or never," said Al-Asari.

Sara and Al-Asari entered the laundry room to find Genevieve Jennings upside down, vigorously rubbing the duct tape around her wrists against the edge of the washing machine.

"Jesus Christ, Sara! Get-me-the-fuck-out-of-here-or-I'm-closing-production-on-this-whole-fucking-show!" Sara peeled the tape off of her mouth, but the rant did not cease. "You're-fired. Everyone's-fired. I'll-have-this-whole-fucking-city-in-jail-if-I'm-not-released-in-five-seconds. Four. Three. Two…"

Sara untied Jennings's ankles and picked up her chair. Jennings sat, collecting herself with deep breaths. "Better," she said. She looked back and forth between Sara and Al-Asari, and landed on Sara. "These aren't fake terrorists, are they?" she asked.

"No, they are not," Sara replied.

Jennings glanced at Al-Asari, then back to Sara again. "This guy—he's a terrorist too?"

"He is," said Sara.

"Did I go on a romantic date with a terrorist?"

"Afraid so."

"Perfect," Jennings said. She turned to Al-Asari. "Son of a bitch! I thought we had something going there!" She shook her head as if it was all a bad dream. "Wow, I am so done with men. My manicurist Luciana was right. You don't meet a man on set."

Sara pulled up video on her iPhone and pressed play. Jennings watched footage of herself in the interview room grabbing the terrorist's machine gun and spraying the room.

"Did I kill him?" she asked.

"It was blanks," Sara said.

"Oh, thank God."

"You were brave," said Sara. "If there had been real bullets, you would have taken out a real terrorist."

"I would have been a hero," said Jennings.

"That's why we showed you the footage," said Al-Asari, stepping in. "You'll need it to repair your career after the scandal."

"Scandal?" Jennings sneered. "What scandal? Sara, why does everyone speak in code around here?"

"We looked through the texts on your cellphone, Ms. Jennings," said Al-Asari. "Couldn't help but come across some awfully naughty correspondence between you and your boss, Glen Gelson."

Blood drained from Jennings's face. Al-Asari scrolled down her Blackberry with a wry smile. "Let's see," he said, reading off the screen. "'I want you so deep inside me, I'd mistake you for my social conscience.' That one I loved. How about, 'You made me so hot last night, I forgot to check the Nielsen ratings.' Pretty wild stuff for a Network GM to be saying to his employee. Tell me, Genevieve, if this gets out, do you think Mr. Gelson will try to save you or himself? Wait, don't answer that."

"Son of a bitch," Jennings seethed.

"Wait, it gets better," Al-Asari said, scrolling down. "'Got my bum bleached for you. How do you like that for taking someone's ass to the cleaners?' This man has three children, does he not?"

"What do you want?" Jennings said through gritted teeth.

"Only your continued cooperation," said Al-Asari. "Business as usual until we are out of here tomorrow afternoon."

"I won't make a peep," said Jennings.

"Good," said Al-Asari. "It is important that you do everything you normally would, right on schedule. For instance, your calendar says you are scheduled to go to the Central Eilat Bank in the morning. Why?"

"Signing some papers." Jennings said. "For release of production funds."

"You will go," said Al-Asari.

"And do what?" said Jennings. "Re-route the money to the Bank of Terrorist Assholes? You think they're going to fall for that?"

"I think they will fall for whatever you ask them to fall for," Al-Asari said. "You will go to the bank and withdraw the money as cash. Bring it to me and these texts will be erased."

"And if I don't?" said Jennings.

Al-Asari tilted her Blackberry towards her. Jpegs of her texts were already attached to an email address: gossip@TMZ.com. "Shall I press send?" said Al-Asari.

"Son of a bitch," Jennings said, deflated. "I'll do it."

"Excellent," said Al-Asari.

"May I please speak to my Co-Executive producer alone for a minute?" Jennings said.

"Of course." Al-Asari walked to the other side of the room.

Sara brought a chair close to Jennings. "Are we insured for this?" Jennings asked.

"The Network is covered," said Sara. "Once the money arrives in Israel, it's the production company's problem."

"Are you a part of this, Sara?" Jennings asked, peering into Sara's eyes. "You've gained a lot from this little catastrophe. I mean suddenly you're in charge. It's suspicious."

"I was captured along with the others," said Sara. "They threatened to start killing us if we didn't do what they said. After they shot Lopez, they went to the call sheet and I was next to answer their demands. Do you think I want to be in this position?"

Jennings held Sara's gaze for a long beat. "Okay, I believe you," she said finally. "Tell me the scenarios. And don't bullshit me."

"Worst case is we all get killed, the terrorists get away with the money, the show's cancelled, and we're all out of a job because we're dead," said Sara. "Best scenario, we have a piece of television history on our hands. You get promoted to SVP for fearlessly leading us to the biggest hit the network has ever seen, the police quietly arrest the terrorists and put them away forever, and Lopez regains any lost funds next season through his massive insurance policy."

Jennings thought about it. "Let's do the second thing."

"Copy that," said Sara.

Al-Asari stepped over. "We all good?"

"Yes."

"Good," said Al-Asari. "And don't worry about the bank getting suspicious. You're not going to take out all the money. Only half. Tell them you want to leave the rest there long term. They'll roll out the red carpet for that kind of American money, and it will make you look like a hero to the Network for thinking fast and saving half the production budget."

"What if I can't do it?" said Jennings.

"I don't know you well enough to say this, but I have a feeling there is no 'can't' for you," said Al-Asari.

Jennings thought about it. "Except for Immanuel Kant," she said.

"Pardon?"

"German philosopher," Jennings said. She rolled her eyes. "Jesus, I am horrible with men. Fine, I'll do it. Now stop messing with my goddamn Blackberry. And would someone please get me that fucking caramel latté?"

Back at the resort, Sara sat at the computer in the main office and dialed up her brother Nathan on Facetime.

"I drew up the plans!" Nathan said excitedly as soon as his face came up. He was in his blue bathrobe, his hair a sleepy mess. "We should have seating like in Minecraft. Bright green and blocky. Look!" Nathan held up elaborate drawings at all angles to the screen. Sara swelled with pride and her eyes got wet.

"I like it," Sara choked.

"Hey, are you crying?" Nathan said.

"Some dust in my eyes."

"You're not getting soft on me, are you, Sara?"

"Never."

"Good, because that would really freak me out," said Nathan. Sara laughed and wiped her cheeks.

Ruti peeked into the room. "Oh, sorry," she said.

"Who's that?" Nathan asked, looking around the Facetime screen. "Is that a girl? Let me see her. Let me see her, Sara!"

Sara waved Ruti in. "This ought to be interesting," she said. "Nathan, this is Ruti. She's a friend."

"Hi, Nathan. It's nice to meet you," Ruti said, angling her face into the screen.

"You're pretty," said Nathan. "She's pretty, Sara. Hey, Ruti, what happened to your neck?"

"An accident. Long time ago. I'm all better now," said Ruti.

"Looks like a panther," Nathan said. Then he looked to Sara. "I like her. Are you going to date her?"

"Little early to tell," said Sara.

"My sister is a good provider," said Nathan. "A little rough around the edges, and stubborn as hell. Plus her feet smell like cheese. Hopefully, you can help there."

"I'm trying," Ruti laughed.

"Ruti?"

"Yes, Nathan."

"What's your opinion of Adele?" he asked.

"I think she is one of the most underappreciated musical geniuses in history. Her top five songs rival the Beatles," she said.

Nathan giggled and spun in his chair. "She's a good one, Sara. Don't mess it up like with the others."

"There were others?" Ruti chided.

"All right, all right, let's get this over with," said Sara.

Nathan turned around and cued the music—this time it was Adele's *Someone Like You.*

"Aw, romantic," said Ruti.

"Cheeseball," said Sara.

And then they sang—the three of them—possibly the corniest pop song ever, right to the end.

When they hung up, Ruti turned to Sara. "Your brother is amazing," she said.

"He's not always like that," said Sara.

"I know. But he's amazing. I love him."

Sara winced. "Look…"

"I don't want to fucking marry you," Ruti said, rolling her eyes. "I just said your brother was cool. So calm down, *metumtam!*"

"I was going to say, 'Nathan seems to like you too.' And that's a big deal."

Ruti searched Sara's eyes. "I believe in you, metumtam. All you've got to do is not screw up."

She kissed her and Sara laughed when Ruti again broke into a heavily accented rendition of Adele's *Someone Like You.*

CHAPTER 9

Tanya was sunbathing on the lower balcony of the cast mansion in a pink bikini as thin as tooth-floss, and with sunglasses big enough to be called goggles. She sipped from a cold glass of mint lemonade daiquiri and chomped on an ice cube.

On the upper balcony, Ramin, the teenaged poet, gazed down on her longingly. He scribbled lines of inspiration into his journal, describing Tanya's soft golden skin, the bleached strands of blond hair on her neck, the sensual arch of her lower back.

Ruti walked out on the balcony with a foamy coffee and gazed out onto the hills.

"Enjoying the view?" she said. Ramin blushed and closed his journal.

"It's okay," Ruti said. "I've had crushes too."

"Does it always hurt like this?" Ramin said. There was desperation in his eyes.

"Depends on your game plan," she said.

"One needs a game plan?" said Ramin.

Ruti sat down across from him, balancing the coffee on her lap. "Well, you can't just write about her all day," she said. "A woman needs to be told. To her face."

"What if she doesn't want to hear it?" Ramin asked.

"Then at least you've tried. But if you don't, you'll never know," said Ruti. Ramin looked unconvinced. Ruti took another sip of her coffee and leaned back onto a pillow. "When I was about your age, I received a letter from my estranged father. He was a famous race car driver and playboy," said Ruti. "He had left my mother and me and my two brothers penniless while he was living in luxury.

"My mother kept him in her heart, even as she slaved away sewing clothes in a factory for shekels a week... even as she got sick. Then I received a letter. My father told me that he was giving me everything—his fortune of untold millions—with one catch: In two months, I was to marry the son of a man to whom he owed many favors—favors that could not be paid off with money."

"What did you do?" Ramin asked.

"I had a sick mother and debt. So I found the boy in a nearby village and I seduced him. I was not in love with him, but I made him fall in love with me, and soon we were married. And then I waited for the money, but it never came. Instead, one day my mother received a letter announcing my father's death. Included was a bill for his casket."

"That can't be," said Ramin.

"I decided to reveal everything to my new husband. I came completely clean about who my father was, the money, the lie that had led me to his village. I pledged that I would make it up to him, that I understood if he no longer wanted me, if he wanted a *gett* [Hebrew for divorce]. But if he chose to keep me, I would be an obedient wife. So he told me: 'I knew all along.' He knew and he didn't care! Every deception he had been aware of since the beginning, but he wanted me anyway."

"That is so beautiful," said Ramin.

"Beautiful? I was horrified," said Ruti. "It stung worse than if he'd hit me. That he could be so dishonest with me that whole time! I could never trust him again. So even though I pledged to stay, I soon left him to become a medic. He's remarried now. Three kids. They live in Tel Aviv. Seems very happy on Facebook."

Ramin was baffled. "But… what does it mean?"

"You don't see?" Ruti said, astonished. "Love is random. God gives us only the power to desire. After that, it is up to you."

As Ramin looked down at his hands, his eyes lit up in epiphany. He smiled for the first time in days. "Thank you, Ruti," he said. "I will never forget you." He hugged her tightly as if he was about to depart on a long voyage. Then he left the patio in a trance.

Sara passed him on the way out. "What was that?" she asked Ruti.

"I told him about a man I once married to pay off a debt. The story inspired him to be brave."

"You were married?"

"Who's to say?" Ruti said, smiling in that cryptic way Sara had come to recognize. "One should never let the truth get in the way of a good pep talk."

Tanya was applying makeup in the mirror when Ramin appeared in her doorframe, panting from his run over.

"You're blocking my light," Tanya said. "If my makeup goes on uneven, I'll end up skewered on *Fashion Police*, so move it or lose it."

Ramin took a step to the side. Tanya pulled open her eyelids for more mascara.

"So, you're just going to stand there, staring at me creepily?" she said. Ramin said nothing. "Suit yourself," she said. "At least allow me this opportunity to school you on the wonders of female face-painting. You'll need to know this someday when you date a girl. This is called base. Gets rid of nasty bumps and zits by turning everything the same color—works wonders on camera. But that's only the start. Then we reach for this little product here. Costs a pretty penny, but it's basically a hangover cure for your face."

"You need none of those things," Ramin said.

"Psht! Someone's never heard of hashtag no filter," Tanya said. "Anyway, are you here to learn or is it time to leave?"

"Your beauty cannot be painted on," Ramin said, his voice filled with passion.

"Oh, go on."

"You have a light, Tanya," Ramin said. "It is bright but flickers under the winds of past hurt. Makeup cannot hide your light and it cannot hide your hurt."

"You don't say?" said Tanya.

"I cannot go back and protect you from the past, but I can shield you today," said Ramin. "Your light is special to me, Tanya. And if you would allow me, I would stay up all night doing nothing but shield your light from the whipping winds."

"Whipping winds? Inner light? Did you drink some of my daiquiri? You know you've got to be twenty-one to consume alcohol."

"I am in love with you, Tanya Lazar. There is nothing a man in love cannot do."

Tanya put down her mascara. She looked over at this scrawny boy, and saw the seriousness in his face. To her surprise, she felt her throat tighten. It was a feeling she mainly experienced when re-watching *The Notebook* on Epix.

"You know I could send you to the hospital with one punch," she said, her voice cracking. "How could you ever protect me?"

The young terrorist walked over to Tanya. He boldly took her hand and got down on one knee. "I swear to Allah, I will protect you, Tanya Lazar, to my dying breath."

In the mirror, to her surprise, Tanya saw her eyes get wet. "Ugh! Now look what you've done. I'm a raccoon."

"To my final breath," Ramin said, eyes ablaze, "I will protect you."

"But you're nothing more than a boy," said Tanya.

"I am your prince," said Ramin. "And you are my queen."

And with that he stood up and kissed her. Ramin tasted bubblegum, apricot lip-gloss, and warm, salty saliva. It was the taste that men cross oceans for. He opened his eyes, drinking in the sensation, and found that Tanya had her eyes open too.

"You're a pretty good kisser for a rookie," Tanya smiled. Then she grabbed his face hard and kissed him again, eyes closed and open mouthed, just as in *The Notebook*.

Tanya took Ramin's hand and led him to her bunk bed. She had a hungry look on her face that Ramin hardly understood, but he tried. It was important that he comprehend each movement, demystify every sensation and lock it away. This was the poetry of life, the beauty of love. He would finally know it from experience.

As he lay down next to her, Ramin looked over to the mirror to witness everything in full view, but what he saw astonished him. In bed, Tanya was a mermaid. She had wavy golden hair, a long curved tail, and gills that breathed. And then he saw himself next to her. But he was no longer a scrawny kid with bony elbows and jet black hair. He was a shark—a mighty gray shark with rows of razor sharp teeth and black eyes.

Ramin blinked and rubbed his eyes, but the shark remained, moving its enormous fin over the beautiful mermaid like a blanket. Ramin tried to fight the vision, but the powerful narcotic of conquest came alive within the boy and could not be denied. No poetry could battle millions of years of genetic destiny. No verse could romanticize the sheer power of having a beautiful woman cede to one's desires. Ramin was a shark now. It scared the living hell out of him...

But it *was* the poetry of life.

CHAPTER 10

Ramin would write an epic poem about her. No, a book of epic poems. No, a trilogy.

Because she gave him the strength to do so. To defy his parents' wishes. To be his own man. Small presses at first, but there might be a mainstream publisher, even an American publisher, interested in a fledgling Palestinian poet. That might be in vogue.

Morning light streaked onto the bunk bed as Ramin lay there gazing at Tanya in wonder and dreaming of their life together. Because she had never completed her makeup ritual, the stark rays revealed pores and blemishes on Tanya's face that Ramin had never seen. He found her even more beautiful.

Their lovemaking, despite the shark that had risen up within him, had been pure poetry. Gentle, deep, and spiritual. A bit quick. And now he could not wait for her to wake up, to begin anew, maybe even to do it again.

When Tanya shifted in bed, he tingled. He wanted to tell her, "My love, I had the most amazing dream. We had a dog—a shaggy dog that had been mistreated, but he lives with us in Bethlehem. We trained him to love, and he learned tricks to please us—he catches tennis balls we toss him. When the baby arrives, he protects her."

When Tanya did finally wake, she lifted her head groggily and checked the clock. Through a blur of exhaustion, she saw that it was a mere six a.m. She slammed her head back down onto the pillow.

"Ugh, daiquiris! Never again," she said, her voice throaty and gruff. "Where am I?"

"You are with me, my love," Ramin said altogether too eagerly. "That's all that matters. You are safe here with me."

Tanya sat up, confused. She looked at Ramin with a sudden sharpness. "You wore a condom, right?" she said.

Ramin nodded. Tanya groaned. She stretched out her arms, pulled on a pair of fluffy baby blue UGG slippers, and went to the bathroom. The door shut. The shower turned on. Ramin sat there for five, maybe ten minutes. He thought to tidy up the bed. Clora, who was listening to her iPod on a bunk across the room, decided to be kind to the young terrorist.

"When that happens, it means you leave," Clora told him.

"Oh, yes," Ramin said. "Yes, of course. Thank you."

"Don't mention it, ya big stud." She tapped her iPod back on and turned away.

Ramin pulled on his pants and walked out of the room and into the cool, crisp morning air. The grass on the hills shimmered with dew. Birds chirped melodic tunes. Ramin touched his stomach and the muscles felt tauter than usual. He did a little dance, then steadied himself, whistling absently when a fellow terrorist walked by with a machine gun.

Ramin coughed low. "Nice morning for a walk," he said quietly.

The other terrorist looked him up and down, saw a condom wrapper stuck to Ramin's shoe, and shook his head. Ramin blushed, picked up the wrapper, and slid it neatly into his journal for posterity.

Back at The Grand Sheba Excelsior, a bloodcurdling screech jolted awake the terrorist guarding the Lopezes. The guard fumbled with his ring of keys and unbolted the supply closet door. Inside, Warren Lopez lay white as a sheet with his head on his wife's lap. His mouth and eyes were wide open, a shocked look of death painted on his face.

"He was bucking, then he stopped!" Sharon sobbed. "You killed him. My husband—you killed him!" The guard grabbed for his walkie. "No!" Sharon yelled. "Get him off me first, you animal. He's heavy and cold."

The terrorist leaned in to lift up Lopez, and that's when they made their move. "Now!"

Sharon brought a pink pepper-spray key chain close to the guard's face and sprayed out its entire contents. The terrorist grabbed his eyes and fell to his knees in agony. Lopez shot up and pried the gun from the terrorist's hands. He then sat on the terrorist while Sharon used several of her silk scarves to tie the terrorist's wrists and ankles. His screams became muffled under a Dolce Gabbana knock-off tied around his mouth.

"He's secure," Lopez said, testing the tightness of the scarves.

Sharon high-fived her husband, then turned to the terrorist. "This is for taking a pregnant woman hostage, asshole!" She kicked the terrorist square in the nuts with her Manolo Blahniks. The terrorist coiled in pain and rolled on the floor.

The couple creaked open the door and tiptoed out into the hall. A terrorist was asleep on a cot with a machine gun lying across his chest. Warren hobbled past him, pointing his stolen gun at the terrorist just in case he woke. In the sparse dawn light, they spotted two guards smoking cigarettes by the front gates. Lopez crouched low and held the gun tight to his chest like some bloated suburban Rambo.

"What do we do now?" Sharon asked, but her husband just shrugged. "You said you had a plan, Warren."

"To get us out of the closet, which I did," said Lopez, triumphantly.

"Great. Classic Warren," Sharon sighed.

In the distance was a van—one of those custom jobs with blacked-out bubble windows and curtains. Was that a naked woman riding a unicorn spray-painted on the hood?

"Walk low," Sharon said.

Warren followed his wife, dragging his bandaged foot through the dirt, careful not to be too loud. They arrived at the van. Sharon tried the front door and it clicked open. They slid low into the front seats. Warren searched the places he'd seen car keys hidden in movies—the glove compartment, under the front view mirror, inside a hide-a-key rock under the seat. Nothing.

"We'll have to hotwire it," Sharon said, as if she'd done it before and it was a pain in the ass. She swiped at her iPhone and pulled up her Survivor Man: Middle East Edition app. "We're going to need wire clippers and a Phillips head."

"Maybe they're here. I'll check," Warren said. He slid through curtains into the back. Sharon scanned for terrorists. Still those smokers by the gate, but no one else yet. The Nordstrom scarves must have held.

"Holy shit, Sharon, there's a waterbed back here," Lopez said. "Hey, we used to have these same sheets."

"A screwdriver, Warren. A screwdriver."

A few minutes later, Lopez slid back into the front with an entire tool case in his lap. "Told you I had a plan. Warren Lopez always has a plan."

"Get down," Sharon said. "That guard's awake. He's headed towards us."

Warren slipped into the back and Sharon followed. They fell onto the waterbed, which squished loudly as water waves swirled under them. Sharon noticed a rusty crack through the side of the van covered with a flimsy strip of duct tape. She peeled back the tape and saw the guard walking directly towards her. She realized that if she pulled her face away from the crack, the light would pour in and reveal their position. She kept herself steady as the terrorist stopped in front of the van.

He unbuckled his pants and took a long, hot piss against the wheel. It was interminable. He moaned and shook when he finally finished. The terrorist then lit a smoke and leaned up against the van, his ass millimeters from Sharon's eyeball. Sharon backed away and replaced the duct tape over the crack ever so carefully. She lay back in bed next to Lopez.

The guard turned towards the van and pressed his face up to the bubble window but couldn't see past the darkened screens and frilly curtains. He pulled at the back doors, but Sharon had not lost the good sense to lock the van when they entered. Eventually, the terrorist climbed up onto the van's roof. The roof lowered several inches under the terrorist's weight as he found a comfortable position to lie down.

As Lopez's heart pounded in his throat, they waited. It may only have been five or ten minutes, but it felt like days until... *snoring.* Loud, deep snoring right on top of them. Sharon took out her iPhone and opened her notebook app:

"#dontwakethebaby," she wrote.

Warren bit his hand so as not to crack up. He took the phone: "Remember when Kale walked in on us having sex and u said: Mommy & Daddy r playing rough and tumble. Haha!!"

"#futuretherapybills," Sharon wrote.

Lopez stifled another laugh, then wrote: "u still luv me?"

"(emoticon wink with lipstick) Unfortunately, yes," Sharon wrote.

Warren nuzzled his wife's neck and kissed her cheek. Just to check, Sharon brushed a hand against Lopez's groin.

She typed: "#alwaysonhard."

A decade before, Sharon had revealed in her wedding

speech that Warren could be headed to the gallows and still might have a semi hard-on.

She typed: "be vewy quiet—I'm hunting wabbits."

Then she placed the phone on her husband's stomach, unbuckled his pants, and let Lopez's long-neglected manhood out to play.

CHAPTER 11

Despite her incarceration in a basement laundry room, Jennings had not ceased giving creative notes on *Natural Dish-aster: Season Five*. She insisted that Sara shoot some "emotional verité," and that meant giving the cast a forum to express their feelings. To cry. Because crying was the key. Yes, they'd need to give context to story and establish a dynamic, but wet faces and snotty criers were supertease necessities, and a campfire session always yielded gold.

So wood logs were set up in a circle and a campfire lit. Flames danced and sparks rose into the air, disappearing into a starry sky. The moonlight was so bright you could almost shoot the scene like that, but klieg lights were brought in nonetheless. The lighting was tasteful, lush.

A man and a woman, both in their fifties and wearing ponchos and colorful beads, sat at the fire's edge, their hair braided like Native Americans. The man had a prominent nose overwhelmed by a lavish beard, and the woman, who was beautiful and dark with bright yellow eyes, wore a wooden necklace with the star and crescent of Islam. The man tapped a conga drum with one hand and the woman rhythmically stirred a shaker as the cast members and terrorists took their seats in a semi-circle around the fire.

Ramin sat next to Tanya; Clora was flanked by Cowboy and Joaquim; Ghana and Nisha shared a blanket, and when Nisha slid a hand on Ghana's knee, it tingled.

"You don't know what you'd be getting into," Ghana whispered to Nisha.

"I have an idea," she replied.

"I'm a mother of two. They're my priority."

"And I'm a twenty-four-year-old adult too scared to come out to my family, let alone admit I've fallen in love with a girl I met on set."

"Maybe you're not ready."

Nisha turned to Ghana. Fire danced in her eyes. "I want to kiss you so bad right now," she said.

Ghana leaned forward, and their quickened breath met inches apart. Ghana slid a hand under the blanket and led Nisha thighward. Their eyes glazed. Both turned back to the strange man and woman in Native American braids so no one would notice.

"Namaste," the man in the poncho said when the producers gave him word. He tapped his drum with one hand as he spoke. "I understand that you have been put at odds with each other in this competition. That you are sworn enemies with different political, geographic, and culinary views. There is tension and misunderstanding between you?" The group nodded. The man's face split into a beatific smile. "Bhiza and I were once like you—we were at odds too. And then... we were not," he said. He squeezed Bhiza's hand, and the group understood her to be his wife.

Then the man pulled his hand away and threw off part of his poncho. Protruding from his left shirtsleeve was a prosthetic arm, smooth and rounded like a dolphin's snout. The one-armed drummer tapped at his conga drum, his thumb and index finger playing a hypnotic beat.

"Yes, we were at odds," he said. "I was a volunteer in a radical Zionist group, urging Israeli expansion into the territories. Bhiza

132

lived in the territories and was the sister of an Islamic radical. It was her job, using her innocent face and dazzling eyes, to get her brother access to highly populated areas without suspicion."

"Ayaaaaa—dangoooooorouuuuuuuus!" The woman, Bhiza, suddenly belted out in song, startling everyone. It wasn't clear if her words were English, or if she understood them, but the result was the same—a hypnotic howl of pain. The man was unfazed. He smiled, winked, and tapped on his drum, his hand rattling like a snake, his eyes closed in blissful meditation.

"Yes, Bhiza and I were who we were. Who knows which was the real terrorist?" he continued. "I saw her in the street one summer day and my heart stopped. So innocent, so beautiful. And she saw me too. And she felt what I felt because she grew so nervous. Right then and there, she dropped her brother's detonation device.

"Love-struck, I didn't even notice what it was. I picked it up and handed it back to her. Then she handed it back to me. I handed it back to her—me, her, me, her—like a suicide bomber hot potato. Ha!" He got a few chuckles from the group, but he was used to a big laugh on that one.

"Heeeeee ggggaaaaaave it baaaayayyayayack," Bhiza sang out.

"Seconds later, there was an explosion from across the street," the man said. "I felt a stinging in my arm and blacked out. But from my unconscious state, I felt a protective hand on me. A tug."

"He feeelt a tuuuuuug."

"I thought for sure I was being taken by terrorists. I assumed I'd be tortured and killed. Truth is, I was not in such bad shape. My arm was cut deep, but God spared me—it was only a flesh wound. In fact, if I was being taken for interrogation, I knew they would tend to my wounds because they would need me alive to get information."

"Neeeeeeed you aaaaaaalive…"

"That's right, if I was a prisoner, I might have gotten the medical attention I needed, and might still have my arm. But Bhiza, bless her, saw me in pain and wanted to save me. So she took me to her village and hid me with her family so I would not be found by her brothers. And I sweated it out. The families tended to me, Bhiza tended to me. Like family. But they did not have the right medical supplies, and had zero medical knowledge, and so, though it was only an infection—*totally solvable* with some antibiotics—I lost my arm in that village."

"He lost his aaaaaaaaaaarm."

"That's right—my good arm!"

"The one he used to druuuuum!"

"But I gained something much more useful that day. I gained an understanding of the people I was once at odds with. Plus, I gained a wife."

"Meeeeeeeeee."

"Let us sing."

"Mayayayayahja!"

Every mouth in the semi-circle opened, seeming to say: "WTF?"

"The point of my story, dear friends, is that togetherness is the key to peace," the drummer went on. "Being amongst the Palestinian people, eating with them, sleeping with them, burying my arm in their backyard—all that made me understand them, and they understood me."

"Heeee turned my brother in to Israeli authoritiessssssss," Bhiza sang out, her face tensing up.

"We must make compromises," said the man, with a tight smile.

"Iiiit was at his wedding ceremonyyyyy."

"I thought we settled that," the man said.

"Not eveeeen close, bucko." Bhiza shot her husband a look so full of venom, you'd have thought he'd die on the spot.

He turned to the cast, his frown smoothing over again into a calm smile. "Seems we have shared a bit too much," the drummer said. "But maybe that's the point. Sharing. Over-sharing even." He shot a look back at Bhiza but didn't seem to make a dent. "Now, let us all share. Share our feelings about those who we are at odds with. Share our anger, our personal disappointment, our rage." He looked over at his wife. "And then throw it away."

"Raaaaaaaaaaaage and disappointment," Bhiza sang.

"Each of you has given me something personal—something that reminds you of that rage." He unfolded a rug and revealed an assortment of objects. Inside were some modern items like clothes and makeup. Some were old, like leather sandals.

"Why is my iPad in there?" said Chrissy.

"This is about sacrifice and absolution," the drummer said. "Who wants to go first?"

In the control room tent, Sara leaned over and kissed Ruti on the neck.

"So this is what turns you on?" Ruti said. "Material sacrifice? I'll keep note."

"Just happy is all," Sara said.

"Me too." Ruti smiled.

At the campfire, Chef Joaquim clutched a pair of oven mitts adorned with a skull-and-crossbones. His eyes were wet as he gazed into the fire.

"Some of you have asked why I got this tattoo with a date on my wrist," said Joaquim. "And I told you it's the date that a friend died. Well, it wasn't a friend, exactly. It was the day I tried to commit suicide." The other chefs listened intently. "I stole a rifle from my old man's shed, got down on my knees, and put the barrel in my mouth... and... and..." He broke down, weeping snot and tears. The producers in the control room high-fived.

The one-armed drummer prodded, "Why, Joaquim? Why

were you there? In that dark place?"

"I kept telling them, 'Don't do this to me,'" Joaquim sobbed. "I pleaded. I called, I wrote letters. Nothing worked…"

"Who? Who didn't listen to your pleas, Joaquim?" asked the drummer.

"The Kitchen Network. Despite everything, they cancelled *Wedding Cake Wizards!*" Joaquim collapsed in a heap of tears, tossing his baking mitts into the fire and then, realizing what he had done, almost leapt into the fire after them. But he pulled himself back, sobbing as he watched them burn. "Where's the fondant?" he yelled at the flames. "Where's the buttercream? And don't tell me cupcakes! Fuck cupcakes! Cupcakes aren't a replacement for cake. They're fucking cupcakes. A child could make 'em. Aahhhhhhh…"

The drummer wrapped his parka around Joaquim's shoulder and sat him back down. "That was great, Joaquim. Really great," he said. "So, who's next?"

In the control room, Sara pulled out her earpiece. "We've hit our tears quota," she said to Ruti. "Let's go make out."

They left the control room tent and stood under the stars. Sara softly touched the panther-shaped scar on Ruti's neck and kissed her.

"You were talking in your sleep again last night," Ruti said between kisses.

"Oh yeah? Anything hot?" said Sara.

"Not exactly."

"Did I mention ex-girlfriends?"

"It was about Nathan," Ruti said. "You kept saying you had the money but that Lopez has to die first."

Sara laughed. "Wow, I've really got some pent-up rage over working such long hours. Help me relieve the tension." She nuzzled Ruti's neck.

"What's even crazier," said Ruti, "is that you were speaking in perfect Arabic."

"That *is* nuts," said Sara, who kept nuzzling.

"You've been pretending not to understand it this whole time," said Ruti. "Why?"

Sara shrugged. "Collecting info. Why should Al-Asari know I can understand his orders?"

Ruti pulled away, a serious look in her eyes. "Do you have something to do with this?" she said. "With Al-Asari—with the terrorists? You would tell me if…"

"Ruti, it was just a dream," said Sara. "We're all under a lot of stress."

"But it has worked out for you, hasn't it?" Ruti said. "This whole terrorist infiltration. You're in charge now. Suddenly, head of the production."

"You think I conspired to shoot Lopez in the foot?" said Sara.

"When we were up above the pavilion in the middle of the night, you popped a pill. You knew you would be doing some public speaking."

"I was nervous. It was an impulse. Are you seriously accusing me of orchestrating a terrorist infiltration?"

"You're not planning on letting them go, are you?" Ruti said.

"All I'm planning to do is get us all out of this alive," Sara said. "Now, can we please continue making out? Because this is seriously killing the mood…"

"I know him, Sara," Ruti said. "I know Al-Asari. From before."

"What are you talking about?"

"He was there in Tel Aviv when the bomb went off, when I was burned on my neck," she said. "I saw his face. He pulled me from the fire, maybe saved me. I swear it was him. I remembered it last night. He did it! He set off that bomb! I know it to be true. And now we have him. We must not let him get away alive. His death will be my justice."

"Whoa! Settle down," Sara said, seeing a frightening faraway look in Ruti's eyes. "Do you know how crazy you sound?"

"The others can try to get away. But I must take my revenge on Al-Asari," Ruti said. "He must die at my hands before he is able to escape."

"Let the police do their job," Sara urged. "I don't want you in danger."

"If he escapes, I will not be able to live with myself. He must die. It is written."

"Ruti, don't do anything crazy. Promise me," said Sara.

"I cannot."

"Ruti, I'll handle Al-Asari. He's going down, I promise you."

Just then a producer ran over. "Sara, shit-show by the campfire. Need you there stat."

Sara took Ruti's hand and looked her square in the eyes. "You asked if I had a plan. And I do. I'll explain everything later. Just don't do anything about Al-Asari. Promise me, okay?"

Ruti nodded. Sara plugged the walkie back into her ear. "Sara, here. What's the trouble?"

At the campfire, Bhiza circled the one-armed drummer with a small, curved blade. "You betrayed Jabbar!" she cried. "He trusted you! We all trusted you!"

"He was a thug," said the man. "He needed to be locked away!"

"And you need to burn in hell!" said Bhiza.

The chefs and terrorists watched in awe as the woman lurched forward and sliced her husband's stomach with the blade. The man looked down, saw the dark blood ooze from his body, and did the only thing a sane person would do: He ran.

"Get back here, you cowardly son-of-a-bitch!" Bhiza screamed. She gave chase, knife in the air. "You betrayed Jabbar. You must pay!"

The producers looked to Sara for direction. "Get everyone in interview," she said. "We need raw emotion. Then right to sleep. No night reality tonight." She turned to the cast. "We need everyone ready for tomorrow's elimination battle. Network's orders. It's going to be a huge day, so get your beauty sleep, people."

Sara snuck off to the main office and dialed up her brother on Facetime. When Nathan's face appeared on the screen, he looked pale, even a little sweaty. Sara wondered for a second if that was her own reflection.

"Hey, buddy," Sara said. "You look like you've been up all night playing Halo."

"Chasing Pavement is the worst song ever written," said Nathan.

"Yup, that's the code," said Sara. "Now turn the video games off."

Nathan eyes widened. "Chasing Pavement is the worst song ever written ever."

"Oh, uh... okay!" Sara's whole body shook. She grabbed for the phone and began dialing Reno police.

"Don't even think about calling the cops," a gruff Russian voice said. A meaty hand shifted the Facetime camera to reveal a rough, flat-nosed man with a deep scar splitting his eyebrow and a prominent neck tattoo. "You must be the sister who sends money. How nice." His voice oozed disdain.

"Who are you?" said Sara.

"I ask the questions," the man said. "All you need to know is your mother owes my boss a debt."

"I'll settle it," Sara said. "Whatever it is. Just leave the house. We can work this out together."

"The debt is substantial. Sixty thousand. Ten more because I have to visit so much. I give you two days, or else."

"Wait. That's too soon," said Sara.

"You'll find a way," the man said. "And no po-po, or else your brother will know what a halo really is."

"If you touch him!" The screen went blank. "Wait, come back!" Sara yelled. She slammed the phone onto the desk. "Goddamn it! Fucking dammit!"

Sara raced out of the office and passed some crew hanging out down the hall. "Where's Al-Asari?" she said. Several people shrugged.

Then a PA said, "I think he's getting that bandage he has on his hand looked at by the medic. Yeah, it got infected. She said she's giving him a tetanus shot or something just in case."

And that's when Sara realized it. Ruti wasn't tending to Al-Asari's wound. She was exacting revenge. Sara sprinted down the hall.

"Something I said?" the PA said, and the crew members laughed.

Sara ran. She ran up the hill, through the resort. She burned her way towards them.

In the Medic's office on the third floor, Al-Asari sat on an examination table, which was covered with a paper sheet. He had removed and folded his jacket and rolled up his sleeves. He was sweating profusely.

"You really think a little dog bite could give me rabies?" Al-Asari said to Ruti. "Seems like the military would want their dogs up to date on shots."

"Do I think it's rabies? Probably not," said Ruti. "But it's inflamed. And it could turn into a nasty infection that could be just as bad."

"I'm uneasy about shots," Al-Asari admitted, closing his eyes and taking short breaths. "I have fainted before. So take it easy on me."

Ruti prepped the needle. She plunged the tip into a small glass vial, then sucked out the clear fluid inside. "You won't feel a thing," said Ruti.

Al-Asari shivered. He took deep hypnotic breaths.

"Just lie down. You can't faint if you're lying down."

"That's what they always tell me," said Al-Asari. "Complete myth."

It was exactly how Ruti wanted him—tense and sweating. Increased blood flow would help get the contents of the needle into his bloodstream to do its work. She milked his nervousness and held the needle in the air, flaunting it. Al-Asari clutched the sides of the table. His eyes darted around the room and his breath sped up. He pulled a locket from his shirt pocket and opened it to the photograph of a young woman. He stared at it and then closed his eyes tightly, as if in prayer.

"Who's the lovely lady?" Ruti asked.

"My wife. She passed, but she used to make me calm every time I feared the needle. But waking up to her face after fainting, that was always the treat."

Ruti, taking Al-Asari's wrist, found a nice, juicy vein. He jerked.

"Steady," she said, "or else we'll have to do it twice."

Al-Asari winced as she plunged the needle into his arm. He went cold as the liquid pushed into his bloodstream.

"Oh, God," Al-Asari said. His sickly face turned pale, his eyes rolled back, and he fell back onto the bed unconscious.

Ruti snapped her fingers in front of his eyes. *Nothing.*

"Goodnight, sweet murderer," she said.

She tossed the needle into the dispenser, and was washing her hands when Sara burst through the door.

"Please, no!" she said, panting. Sara saw Ruti, then Al-Asari lying motionless and white as a bed sheet. "It's over," Sara said, hands over her face. "It's all really over."

Ruti gave her a quizzical look.

"You didn't have to do that," Sara continued. "He wasn't all bad. He was just…" Sara fell to her knees. She leaned over a small waste paper basket and vomited. "Oh gawd…"

Ruti rolled her eyes. "Now I have two big babies in my clinic."

Sara wiped vomit from her chin and looked up in horror. *Ruti was a cold-blooded killer, and she was making a joke?* Sara vomited some more. Everything was lost. Sara would have to improvise. There was an air rifle in the office cabinet. She'd have to take them out one by one. But even then, there would be no hope. All was lost, all was lost…

"Oh, I am so embarrassed," Al-Asari moaned. His face was a jaundice yellow and shiny with sweat. "I can't believe I fainted… again."

"You weren't kidding," smiled Ruti. "You should take a Xanax next time. Here, have some water."

"Thank you," said Al-Asari, slurping gratefully at the paper cup. He noticed Sara on the floor. "Ms. Sinek, what are you doing here?"

Sara's mouth was agape. "I-I-I…"

"We will have to watch that hand," said Ruti. "Just keep it clean and dry."

"Thank you, Doctor," Al Asari said. "I feel better already. And thank you for being so gentle with me."

"You're welcome, my dear," said Ruti.

Al-Asari stood up shakily and walked toward the door. He looked down at Sara and the vomit-splattered trash basket, and wrinkled his nose. "You ate the babganoush, didn't you? Disgusting," he said.

Al-Asari walked out and it took a full minute for Sara to pull herself together. "But I thought…"

"Don't be an idiot," Ruti said. "Besides, I stole his ID card when he fainted, so now I know where he lives. Al-Asari gets a pass this time, but I will kill him and eventually his entire family too. There will be no mercy whatsoever."

Sara gulped.

Tough Israeli chick.

CHAPTER 12

A stack of pizza boxes and Diet Cokes awaited the cast back at the mansion. They all groaned.

"Jesus Christ, again?" Chef Nisha said.

"Fuck it, I love pizza," said Joaquim.

But then they smelled something other than the melted cheese and cheap tomato sauce—an earthy sweetness that could only come from authentic Middle Eastern cooking. Hints of cumin, za'atar, chives, the sizzling of fried onions and lamb. It was an aroma that bespoke a long culinary tradition.

The cast bee-lined for the kitchen like a mob of famished zombies. There they witnessed a sight they hadn't seen in a long time, and some had never seen: a cook engaged in the pure joy of making food. No clocks, no screaming executive chefs or expediters, no incessant buzz of a restaurant ticket machine, no haughty waiters or picky customers returning dishes for lack of seasoning. Just joy.

Salid's movements were breathtaking—his eyes were closed and his nostrils wide to take in the aromas of his cooking. He stopped only to consider a taste, to add spices or peppers, to upgrade flavor or texture. Minced lamb sizzled in bulgur crust. On the stove, lentil stew simmered with red peppers, dill, garlic, and cumin. Turnips stuffed with rice, flavored with cloves, garlic, and cardamom, baked slowly in the oven. Eggplant with pomegranate seeds and garlic cooled under a fan next to fried dough balls stuffed with meat, pine nuts, and onions. The aromas were beyond tantalizing.

"Pavlov don't know shit about salivating," Cowboy said.

When Salid turned to take his cauliflower out of the oven, he opened his eyes to the sight of a pack of primal wolves. He knew just what to do. He quickly doubled and tripled his recipes. He pulled out bags of fresh eggplant and tomatoes; he laid ingredients out in place. As if under hypnosis, the chefs all picked up paring knives, chopping, dicing, and seasoning what Salid set out for them.

"Oil the eggplant just barely," Salid instructed softly. "The natural oils are tastier. And don't pull the seeds. They make it less bitter."

The chefs obeyed every word.

"Deconstructed nothing. This is real food," said Ghana. "Simple, earthy, flavorful. God's food."

On the table, big wooden bowls overflowed with fattoush salad, and small plates were set out with pickled cucumbers, black olives, hummus-ful, grilled zucchini with za'atar, and labenah cheese. The cast, ordinarily wild animals in the sight of such delicacies, waited patiently for Salid to finish plating and to join them.

"You honor us with this table tonight," said Chef Clora. She pulled out a seat for Salid at the head of the table. "To the chef," she said, and raised her glass.

"To the chef!" they all sang out. And then they dug in.

For minutes, only moans, slurping, and the hurried clanks of forks and plates could be heard. The food was eaten slowly, the chefs savoring each sumptuous morsel. Knowing smiles were exchanged, eyes rolled in bliss, and heads shook in disbelief.

Nisha broke the silence. Her head was bowed almost in prayer. "Sometimes I forget why we do what we do, you know?

This food brings it all back. It's about love."

"Love," the others repeated.

"And friendship," said Tanya.

The feasting continued until curiosity got the better of Etienne. "Salid, what is the flavor combination coating on the lamb?" he said. "I've never tasted anything like it before. And yet it's familiar."

"A sumac mixture?" guessed Chrissy.

"More lush. Tarragon?" asked Cowboy.

"More aromatic."

"Salid. C'mon, dude," said Chef Joaquim. "What's the secret? I'll pay you for it."

"I am afraid that is impossible," Salid said.

"C'mon! Everyone has their price," said Joaquim. "I pull in bank at L'Apicio—I've got cheddar to spend, bro. And I won't tell. Cooks' honor."

"Better give him what he wants, Salid, or he'll never shut up about it," said Tanya.

"C'mon, Salid, spill the beans," said Etienne. "We won't tell a soul…"

"It's called Ikhaz'a," Salid finally said.

"It's like a spice?" asked LizZ. "A weed?"

"A hybrid," said Salid.

"Called it," said Chrissy.

"Where do you get it?" asked Ghana. "I have a client who would go mad for this. Cash on the table."

"I'm afraid that no amount of money can purchase Ikhaz'a," Salid said. "Because Ikhaz'a no longer exists."

"Now he's messing with us," said Etienne.

"That, or he's going to be super fucking rich," said Clora.

"If it were only so," Salid said with a bittersweet smile. "You see, Ikhaz'a requires a certain kind of volatile environment to grow."

"Extreme arid climates?" said LizZ.

"That seems to help," said Salid. "What it needs most of all, actually, is oppression."

"You lost me, bro," said Joaquim.

"I am from a small town right on the border," said Salid. "Nearby is a military zone that is restricted both to Palestinians and to Israelis—kind of a no-man's land. After the second Intifada, Israel extended the border to put a buffer between the two lands. To do so, they had to bulldoze certain villages, cutting down trees to clear the way for their tanks. I guess they wanted to make sure no one was hiding. And so they cut down rows of olive and citrus trees along the wall.

"When the tanks began rolling through, soldiers would chew sunflower seeds and toss the unopened ones on the ground. My theory is that the seeds took root amongst the burnt roots of the olive and citrus trees, and there was a mix. It took years, but the seeds came to life. And when they did, ugly, smelly plants sprouted. Try to eat them off the ground and you'll be sick—smells like sewage. But when ground up and roasted, they become earthy and aromatic unlike anything I have tasted on earth.

"I have tried to replicate this outside of that environment. I have planted sesame next to olive and citrus, and waited and waited—but it never is the same, never right. Israel has now tightened the security in the zone by the border, so there is no longer a way to sneak in. Months ago, I saw that, for the benefit of their tanks, they paved the area that had the Ikhaz'a plant. So, no more Ikhaz'a. What you are eating is actually the very last of it in existence. You are the last people on earth to taste it."

The chefs were in awe. They gazed down at their plates, at their forkfuls of food, and paused. This was an historic moment in culinary history.

"Where I am from is not unlike what you experience in some ways," said Salid. "People our age, we want things. We have dreams. We watch TV and we want it all. My brother Rafi—he dreams of being on *American Idol.* My uncle Yvar? He longs to play tennis against Rafael Nadal. But the situation makes that impossible. And it is not the war. War you can understand. It is the nature of our relationship with Israel. The humiliation of the check points, the blockade that makes it so we cannot depend on the basics we need to live.

"Little boys who would grow up to be something—doctors, teachers, lawyers, writers—they are treated like criminals. They sense the fear and desperation of their parents—the anger, too. Education is a luxury when families are scrambling to survive. The Jewish people have been persecuted around the world for thousands of years, and then were offered a homeland.

"I, too, would protect it to the death, but there is cruelty happening. We are given identification cards and, if you make a mistake, you earn a green dot on your card—that means no entry into Israel. Which means that soldiers can come to where you live and interrogate you. They can jail you for nothing. Who can live under such stress? Who can build a career and find love, or thrive as a singer, a tennis player… or a chef?"

Salid paused to look around the table. "You may have noticed that I close my eyes when I cook. Sometimes it is to use my other senses, but more often it is to imagine that some day I will be free. To walk amongst people like you who are not suppressed or unemployed or frustrated. And yes, people who are not violent. Because when a wall blocks you from freedom, you bang against that wall —and even if it hits you back twice as hard, you keep hammering at it, because what choice do you have but to keep on trying?"

That night as Tanya lay in bed, Ramin, using a quill and a

bottle of ink, wrote a poem on her naked lower back.

"Is this like the poet's version of a tramp stamp?" said Tanya.

"Concentrating," said Ramin.

"It tickles. What does it say?"

"It is about love."

"Sure. Then someone's going to translate and it'll be like, 'Tanya craves cock' or something."

"Please," said Ramin. "I am working. Think about something else."

"I am. I was. I can't get what Salid said tonight out of my mind, actually. About being free to thrive. He's such a talented guy. In the States, he'd get a gig anywhere he wanted, at the very least as chef de cuisine. Is what he described what your life is like too?"

"It can be frustrating to be told you cannot do the things you want to do," said Ramin. "But this is, to a degree, the same everywhere in the world."

"What do you want to do?" asked Tanya.

"I am doing it," said Ramin. "Now let me concentrate."

"Okay," said Tanya. "So, this is going to sound pretty spoiled right now, and you're not listening anyway so I'm just going to say it. On a weird level, I kind of relate to Salid. I mean, I sometimes feel like a prisoner. Instead of soldiers, there are these producers encouraging me to act like someone I'm not. My dad worked for twenty-three years at an insurance firm and, then one day, he was laid off, for no reason at all. I watched him come home with his pathetic little cardboard box of framed photos and paperweights. He was so stunned he just sat there for months until his unemployment insurance ran out. Still sitting there, actually.

"My mom doesn't know what to do with him and she's not about to bust out into the workforce. Meanwhile, people are offering me ten grand just to hang out at some club for the night. They don't even want me to cook anymore. Just hang out and get blasted. Sometimes I wish there was a parent around, to just be like, 'No, go to your room. You're barely twenty-six years old and you know what? You're grounded.'

"But instead everyone is like 'Go! Go!' and I don't want to disappoint them. I mean they hire me and there's a ton of chefs who beg for my gigs. But sometimes I'm like, 'When is it going to end exactly?'... Ouch! Too hard!"

"Sorry."

"I know I sound like an asshole," Tanya said, "but when we were all just sitting around and eating and talking, it was almost like I was a regular person and I was among family. Is it like that for you ever? Just sit with people and eat and talk and not feel the need to get all fucked up and crazy on drugs."

"All the time," said Ramin.

"I'd like that, you know. I think I want that life. Not saying white picket fence in the 'burbs, but like, friends and brunch and . . . I don't know, it just felt so right," Tanya said.

Ramin smiled. It was exactly the wish he'd inscribed on Tanya's lower back in poem form—for her to want a normal, slow life, full of love and family. A life with him.

"Tell me about your life, Ramin," said Tanya. "Tell me every-thing. Your parents, siblings, what street you live on. What kind of toothpaste you use. I don't want you to leave out one detail."

"All done," said Ramin. He put the cap back onto the ink bottle and laid down his quill. He grabbed Tanya's hand mirror. "Go ahead," he said. "Read it."

Under the veil of night, Etienne and LizZ snuck into the kitchen. They laid out the new ingredients Etienne had scribbled onto his napkin, including ground mastic, orange blossom water, ricotta cheese, ground nutmeg, and one more they'd simultaneously come up with at the beach: 1 tablespoon of *mahlab*. They worked slowly and deliberately, their hands moving as if attached to one body. It took nearly two hours to prep, and when it was ready to bake, the sun, blood orange and delicious, had begun to rise above the sea.

"That's everything," said Etienne.

"Our baby," said LizZ.

The two chefs peered into the oven like anxious but exhausted parents in a maternity ward.

"What shall we call her?" said LizZ.

"Junk," said Etienne.

"La Junk," LizZ corrected. "Americans love that French shit."

"Oh, you are so very naughty ..."

"Oh, you are sooo naughty," Nisha sighed. Sheets twisted across her naked, sweaty body.

Ghana gazed up at the ceiling fan as if it confused her. "That was..."

"Everything," said Nisha.

"That," Ghana said, nuzzling up against Nisha's neck, "was only the start."

Back at the resort, Sara, in bed with Ruti, ran fingers through Ruti's thick curls and kissed her forehead.

"Tell me a bedtime story," Ruti said, yawning.

"That's yawn number two," said Sara. "You're not going to

make it through so much as a haiku."

"You've slept in my bed three times and you already know my yawn count?"

"It's pronounced."

"You know who used to count my yawns? *(yawn)* My dad. You remind me of him in many ways."

"That's not weird at all," said Sara.

"You both wear lavender deodorant," Ruti said, sleepily, "and you both *(yawn)* count my yawns. And you are both stubborn like, like… *sloths.*"

And then she was asleep, her mouth opened slightly, a gentle whistle coming from her nose. Sara again kissed Ruti's forehead and lay back on her pillow. "Night, my dear." She peeled open a trashy magazine and tried to settle into the celebrity photos, but couldn't manage any joy. It was Ruti's mention of her father that kept Sara so distracted. Al-Asari had been right about Sara's involvement in his death. How he knew, Sara couldn't possibly imagine. The IDF's cover-up had been thorough and deep.

Still, Sara couldn't forget that awful night. It had rained so hard it hurt the skin, rained so hard the plump drops pinged off the tank's hull like bullets. There were five of them, all packed into the Merkava Baz battle tank that evening. Sara sat in the gunner turret staring at a tiny screen. Whenever heat of any kind showed up—a dog, a vehicle, a terrorist with a Russian-made anti-tank missile—a black spot appeared on the screen.

Dv'or, the stocky tank commander, sat wedged in the commander hatch. Idan, whose weed habit had earned him the nickname *Mastool* (stoned), was in the cannon loader's hatch. And "Stinky" Yuri, who claimed he had food poisoning but everyone knew was just chicken-shit, continuously passed gas from the driver's hatch. All four soldiers wore flak jackets, heat-seeking goggles, and intra-tank communication helmets.

But there was also a fifth person in the tank, or as Yuri and

Dv'or liked to call him, The M.R.S. (murderer/rapist/sonofa-bitch). MRS, a bearded Syrian with a thick unibrow in a brown prison jumpsuit, sat low in the turret, wrists and ankles cuffed and immobile. MRS was there because, on top of murder and rape (which eyewitnesses confirm he one-hundred-per-fucking-cent committed), he also copped to knowing the whereabouts of a certain cabal of scientists who were at that moment putting the finishing touches on chemical weapons intended for both Israeli and American targets.

Sara had retrieved the information from the prisoner, who let her know that he would lead them to the precise location of the scientists, but only if Sara went along for the ride. Every active Merkava Baz battle tank in the Israeli army housed a stack of depleted uranium 120-millimeter missiles, a bushel of hand grenades, two MAG machine guns, a crate of 5-caliber shells, and five-hundred 35-millimeter bullets. But not this tank.

And there was one uniquely fucked-up reason why. In order to fit the murderer/rapist/sonofabitch into the tank, they had to forego the MAG ammunition and the crate of shells. This was a simple point-and-shoot operation with the cannon. They weren't supposed to need the rest. But what if they did? This MRS sat where the bullets were supposed to be, and that made Yuri, Dv'or, and Idan hate the bastard even more.

The rain slowed as the tank rolled across the Gaza border and into enemy territory. That wasn't necessarily good news. Though it allowed Sara better vision through her periscope, and thus a greater likelihood of accurately aiming the cannon, it also afforded any number of masked assholes with Russian Agger anti-tank missiles better vision as well, and at last count there were plenty of those about. Idan, Dv'or, and Sara tried not to think about that, and luckily there were other issues to be royally pissed about, chief among them Yuri's flatulent stomach and the broken AC system.

"Goddamnit, Yuri, are you shitting your pants? It smells like a dog's balls died in here."

"*Abal.* I told you my stomach has knife pains."

"Then go on sick leave."

"If I go on sick leave, I miss Illil's visit. She's here Tuesday."

"So you're waiting to shit in front of your girlfriend? Let me give you some advice, *metumtam*: Chicks don't dig that. Ask Sinek."

"I can confirm," Sara said. "Chicks don't like shitty boyfriends. And they hate shitting boyfriends. Now can you please both *shotk?*"

"You heard her, Yuri," said Idan. "Plus, you're breaking the Geneva Convention gassing our shithead prisoner."

"Who gives a shit about this MRS?" yelled Yuri. "He's dead the minute we bomb these *fuckim.*"

"Guys, give it a rest. I can't think," said Sara. She gazed at her yellow screen, willing herself to concentrate.

How Sara had even gotten this deep into the IDF was a crazy, long story. Her U.S. battalion had been safely stationed in Turkey when Sara got the call to visit the Sergeant Major's office. It was an odd call. Officers of Sara's rank were rarely in the presence of a Sergeant Major, unless it was to be disciplined. Sara's bunkmate dragged a thumb across her throat to indicate that Sara was *S.O.L.* When Sara entered the office and was met not only by the Sergeant Major but by a tall, meticulous-looking woman in an Israeli military uniform, she knew it was true. Sara saluted.

"At ease, Sinek," said the Sergeant Major.

"Sir," said Sara.

"Sinek, I'd like to introduce you to Lieutenant Safit. She's been hard at work gathering intelligence on Gaza, and some significant crossover has come to her attention—activity that points to plans for an attack on American bases, and even localized spots in the United States. Now I don't have to tell you how important our interests are in the region."

"No, sir."

"Then you understand how valuable it would be to have someone embedded over there with our allies. To look after our interests. To do some digging on the threats to our nation."

"Yes, sir, but as you may know…"

"Your knowledge of the language and local culture, in addition to your religious background, make you a perfect candidate. I would think you'd be especially keen to help out."

"Sir, my religion is not a factor in…"

"I'm not saying that, goddamnit. Relax, Sergeant. Your religion is the U.S. Army. So whether you're a Jew, a Christian, or a goddamn Scientologist, you're here to protect U.S. interests."

"Yes sir, Sergeant Major."

"Now tell me: How's your brother doing? Nathan his name is?"

"Struggling, sir," said Sara. "And that's why it's so important that I—"

"I'm aware you've had some financial problems back home, that it's important for you to feel that your brother is taken care of, and that you're scheduled to head back there next month."

"In twelve days, sir…"

"I admire your commitment to family," said the Sergeant Major. "But you're needed here, Sinek. Now, to help you out, we would consider this a special combat mission. You'll receive imminent damage pay as well as hazard pay right off the bat, even if you find yourself pushing pencils for the next six months. Bet your brother could be helped by that kind of additional compensation."

"Yes he could, sir. Thank you, sir."

"Good. Then it's settled," said the Sergeant Major, looking pleased. "You must have a bunch of questions for Lieutenant Safit here?"

Sara turned to the Israeli Commander. "When do we ship out?" she asked.

Three years of chasing dead-ends preceded by what appeared to be a final breakthrough. The MRS (his real name was Hasan Amami) had spent three years in Michigan, where he was wanted not just for suspected terrorist activity, but also for the alleged rape of a college girl, so Sara was called in to see if she could get anything out of the guy. The prisoner had already been through days of Israeli interrogation, so Sara took the good cop approach and brought him a cup of thick Turkish coffee and a plate of *grhaybeh* sugar cookies.

And he talked. Sara was surprised at how quickly. He described the scientists, their faces, the inside of their homes and lab. He knew the type of 3-quinuclidinyl benzilate nerve gas they were producing, that it was the kind of gas that literally melts your face off. All the info checked out with Intelligence. The MRS' only request was to avoid super max so he could earn visits from his family. That request had been approved upon the confirmed kill of the scientists and the termination of their lab. "Kill the brains and the body will die. Is that the theory, Sergeant?" the prisoner said to Sara, as he ate the last cookie. "Makes good sense."

The tank slowed next to a burnt-out warehouse near a residential street lined with apartment buildings. The war had taken its toll on the roads. Stray dogs darted between overturned cars with shattered windows. Sara flinched every time a black blob shot across her yellow screen, only to confirm that it was yet another mutt. "I swear to God, these dogs had better smarten up or they're going to get shot."

"We've arrived," said Yuri as the tank came to a stop.

Sara poked out of the gunner's hatch with her night vision goggles: a street away, a row of shabby apartment buildings. Candles lit a room on the third floor corner. Sara leaned down into the turret. "Describe it," she said to the prisoner.

"The building has four stories," he said. "There's a rusty pipe along the middle. On top there are many television antennas."

"Motherfucker just named every shitty apartment in Jabalia!" shouted Idan. "I'm telling you, if this is some bullshit, I will personally chop his nuts off."

"The largest antenna has green spray paint on the wall behind it—SpongeBob SquarePants," added the prisoner.

"Okay, his nuts are definitely coming off…"

Sara spotted the spray-painted cartoon character through her binoculars. She came down into the turret. "I'm going to lift you up with some binoculars. I need you to tell me exactly which apartment it is, okay?"

The terrorist nodded. Sara placed night-vision goggles on his head and pulled him up through the hatch. "That them?" Sara asked.

"The rain… makes it hard," said the prisoner.

"I told you this MRS is full of shit. Let's just kill him now and head back out of this hellhole."

"The candles near the window," Hasan said. "Three levels up. I see them there. Fullah, Zogby, and Khoury. I see them there. I swear to Allah."

"How you can be sure?"

"Fullah is fat and is stuffing his face even now," said the prisoner. "He has no beard. Zogby always wears that baseball cap. New York Mets."

"He's playing you, Sinek," said Idan.

"Then Khoury. He wears an eye-patch even though he has twenty-twenty vision. Apparently, he thinks it makes him look tough, but he's a total coward."

Sara pulled the prisoner back into the turret. She stood up through the hatch and looked through her binoculars. "Hasan, who's the fourth guy?" she asked.

"I do not know that man," said the prisoner.

"He's clean shaven as well. How many men in this area have no beard?"

"He is likely a new scientist. They tend to assimilate so they can travel."

"Two for the price of one!" said Idan. "Let's blast 'em."

"Or he's a national," said Sara.

"No, he's not one of us," Idan said. "Why would an Israeli be here so deep in the *shukarim* hanging out with jihadists? That's just stupid."

But Idan had heard the same rumors as Sara. The Gaza border lockdown had caused chaos. Visiting Israelis rushed to get out, but there was danger at the border from both IDF and Hezbollah. Confusion made it impossible to pass. According to rumors, hundreds of Israelis were still within Gaza walls. But where?

"I'll call it into base," said Sara. "If there's an Israeli in the building, mission's off."

"My stomach," Yuri complained, and the tank again filled with his flatulence. "I have to shit. I'm not lying."

"Yuri, shut the fuck up."

"I held it long enough!" he protested. "It's now or I shit in the tank."

"Open the side hatch," said Sara. "Could be a few minutes before base gets back to us on this."

"You better hope you don't shit on a land mine or the first thing that gets blown off is your *beitsim*," said Dv'or.

Yuri opened the side hatch. He hung off the side of the tank, groaning. Sara looked again through her binoculars and saw one of the candles on the third floor being blown out. "They're moving," she said.

"Could be onto us," said Dv'or.

"Or they could be going to sleep," said Idan. "It's past midnight."

"It's them. I swear to you," the prisoner said. "You must do it now."

"Shut him up, goddamnit! Yuri, get back in here."

"A second."

The rain started up again, this time harder than before. Sara got back into the tank and again radioed in. "Raim One to Base: Anything yet? They may be on the move."

A flood of static accompanied a voice that came back over the radio. "We've determined low probability of an Israeli national in there. Your order is to proceed as planned."

Sara dropped the radio. "Ninety-six meters close," she said to Dv'or.

"Load up," Dv'or instructed.

"Loaded," said Idan. "Lock it."

"Locked," said Sara.

"Yuri, get in here now and shut the damn hatch!" shouted Dv'or. "We're doing this."

Base responded through the static: "Shoot to kill," they said. Sara peered into the periscope, finger steady on the trigger. Blood pounded in her temples. She lined the target up in the crosshair. Being just half a millimeter off could mean the wrong apartment. She leaned in. "Yuri, get in here!"

A blast. But not from the cannon. Gunfire blasted the tank from across the road, bullets exploding off the hull. Sara pulled off her target, swiveling the periscope. Shooters behind the overturned cars. "We're seen!"

"I'm shot!" Yuri yelled, pulling himself back into the tank. Blood spread across his pant leg. "They shot me in the fucking ass!" Yuri leaned back in to close the hatch. But before he could, the prisoner sprang up from the turret. He stumbled forward onto Yuri, and they both fell out of the side of the tank, hard onto the muck and rocks.

"Yuri! Goddamnit!"

The prisoner struggled to his knees, wrists held up in the air to show the attackers that he was one of them. Yuri scrambled up and tackled him, getting on top of the prisoner and holding him down with his knees as he went for his handgun. Then a bullet struck him in the neck. Yuri touched the hot blood there and collapsed face down in the muck. The terrorist clambered up again. "Brothers! Save me!" he called out. But the response came in bullets, blasting through the prisoner's stomach. He collapsed.

Dv'or pulled the hatch closed. "Fire at the goddamn target, Sinek!" he yelled.

Sara shifted the gunner again. Through the periscope, she could see a second candle flickering on the third floor of the apartment building. Sara could still make them out. Four men, not three, as weeks of intelligence had suggested. *Four. But who? Who the fuck was in there and why?* No time to find out. Sara leaned onto the trigger.

"Fire!"

The cannon erupted and the apartment lit up, the entire third floor exploding. Fire, debris, and dust obscured the view through the periscope. Sara swiveled the gunner back to the attackers and unloaded what ammo she had, spraying the blobs, which went black in her yellow screen.

When the incoming gunfire thinned, she waited. "C'mon, you fuckers…"

Two black blobs headed in different directions on her screen. Sara spun the gunner left and nailed the first runner, then shifted right, finger hard on the trigger, until she emptied her chamber. There was silence. No movement on her yellow screen.

"Is it clear?"

"Who the fuck knows?" said Sara. She lifted the side hatch, jumped out of the tank, and into the pounding rain and muck below. Yuri lay dead next to the prisoner. Sara checked Yuri's pulse, but he was gone. She turned to the prisoner. He coughed blood onto his beard, his unibrow scrunched like a bat on his forehead. But he was alive.

"Be still, Hasan," Sara said, tying a belt around his stomach to stem the bleeding. "I'm going to get you out of here."

"I cannot move," he said, weakly.

"You fulfilled your part of the deal. Now let me do mine." Sara went to lift him, but the prisoner winced in pain and waved her off.

"A second. I must rest a second."

"It's all we've got," Sara said. She rested the prisoner's head on her lap.

"Did we get them?" the prisoner asked.

"You got them, Hasan. You did a good job."

The prisoner grinned. "Then he is dead. My cousin is dead."

"One of the scientists was a cousin? Why didn't you tell me that?"

"*Scientists?*" the prisoner said, coughing more blood. "I don't know any scientists."

"Yes you do," said Sara, uneasy. "Fullah, Zogby, Khoury. Dead. It's why we're here."

"Probably friends from the Israeli hotel where my cousin works," he said, "though I can't imagine the man with the eye patch gets much front-desk work." Managing a chuckle, he looked up at Sara. "Fat bastard stole my wife. Then he called the police on me. It's why I fled to America. But I got him. Praise be, I got my revenge…" A sickly smile formed on the prisoner's lips as Sara looked on in horror. He coughed a big gob of blood onto his beard. Then his face went slack.

"Sinek! We've got company!" yelled Dv'or.

Half a dozen men with machine guns appeared behind the overturned cars and stepped out into the open. Sara grabbed Yuri and dragged him back into the tank.

"We move!"

Sara got in just as bullets rained down on the tank and she slammed the hatch shut. Yuri's body dropped into the turret, limp and soaked with blood, rain and muck. Idan jumped into the driver's hatch. Sara got in the gunner hatch and the tank lurched forward, crushing the remains of the *murderer/rapist/ sonofabitch* who had masterminded a genuine Gazan clusterfuck, and speeding out onto the road under heavy gunfire.

CHAPTER 13

In the back of a custom van, to the sounds of a terrorist alternately yawning and peeing off the roof, Warren and Sharon Lopez awoke sweaty and parched on a waterbed. Sharon had already been up for twenty-three minutes, per her internal clock, which paid no heed to international time zones. She held a finger to her lips after her husband rustled awake. She held up her iPhone: "We got 2 go."

Lopez nodded. The terrorist jumped off the roof and headed back into the pavilion, his Uzi hanging loosely over a shoulder. He was met by another terrorist—the one who'd been tied up in the supply closet. He waved his arms dramatically and scolded the sleepy terrorist in rapid-fire Arabic. The two split up, hunting for the married couple they would surely kill if they discovered them.

"I miss Kale," Lopez whispered and almost broke down in tears thinking of the boy.

Sharon hopped off the waterbed and scanned a small crack in the door. Guards were everywhere.

Their only chance was to get the van going and blow past them. Blow right out of the gate. Sharon grabbed the screwdriver.

"It's time," she said.

Lopez nodded. He was all in.

In the peaceful morning light, the cast of *Natural Dish-aster* awoke, their bellies full of deliciousness and their minds full of newfound enlightenment. There were no broken bottles anywhere, no overturned ashtrays or vomit piles, not even any cameras there to document cranky hangover wake-ups. Their sleep had been peaceful and deep. Several of the chefs and terrorists sat up on the balcony sipping cups of thick Turkish coffee and looking out at the hills. Ghana served persimmon lemonade with freshly picked mint.

The terrorists pointed out native birds, and Tarik did a perfect imitation of a Northern Gannet. Local radio played an entire album by Oum Kalthoum, the Nina Simone of the Middle East. A gentle hookah was packed and smoked, and soon terrorists and chefs alike were giggling and patting each other on the back. It was a slow morning.

"I'm going to miss you, dude," Joaquim said to Sheik.

"I won't forget you either," replied Sheik.

"You guys on Facebook?"

"Facebook is for geezers," said Sheik with a chuckle. "Check my Instagram for the good shit."

Everyone laughed at that. #bestmorningever.

"Dude, I got the munchies like a mutherfucker," said Joaquim.

"I hear that," said Chrissy. "Any more of that dope hummus left from last night?"

"Dude, I licked that bowl clean ages ago."

"My kingdom for something crunchy," said Clora.

Etienne and LizZ emerged from the kitchen carrying a large platter covered with a napkin. The aroma emanating from therein was buttery and earthy and sweet, like brown sugar had French-kissed a field of cardamom. The room went silent. LizZ removed the napkin with a flourish, revealing a row of bird-shaped pastries that were flaky and robust.

"We call it *La Junk*," she said.

"You could call it *Le Penis* and I'd still eat the whole damn tray," said Sheik.

"Ha, you crazy!" said Joaquim who patted Sheik on the back.

Everyone took a pastry, and the sound of layers of crust into sweet cream, and then back into crust, then jam/crust/spiced nuts/salty crust/sweet cream/savory crust materialized as heavenly sighs and lascivious moans.

"But... how?" Tarik said, eyes wet. "How were you able to get it so crunchy, then so creamy, then there's like crunch underneath that, but then there's ... what? Is that jam and ...?" Unable to finish his sentence, he pushed the crumbs at the corner of his mouth back onto his tongue.

"Cream/crunch/jam/crunch/nuts," added Clora, like she was listing off the five wonders of the culinary world. "It's like sufgayot did a three-way with baklava and Mom's peach cobbler. And they all came at the same time."

"You're like a poet," said Sheik. "You should, like, rap."

"I want to," Clora said, stuffing the rest of the pastry into her mouth and eyeing the platter for another.

Etienne and LizZ sat. They each took a pastry and bit in. The crunch/cream/crunch/jam/spice/crunch/nuts taste the others spoke of hit hard. Their eyes glazed over as if they'd slurped mercury water. Both sunk into their chairs, spreading oceans between their thighs.

LizZ managed a grin. "You are a very bad man," she mouthed to Etienne.

"And you, my friend, are Anne Burrell," said Etienne. Then their shoulders went slack.

Ramin emerged from Tanya's room, the sweet exhaustion of post-coital bliss slowing his every step. He'd been drained of his essence (more than once, he was proud to admit), and yet was alight with poetic inspiration. Thanks to Tanya, he could see his entire future ahead, and it glimmered.

Two gloved fists grabbed Ramin's shirt and threw him roughly against a wall. "*What the—*" A glove went over his mouth that smelled like wet leather. Ramin struggled. His attacker wore a mask, but it wasn't one of the men from his group.

"Stop! Help!" Ramin said, straining through the glove. Then he bit down on the hand. *Hard.*

"Hot damn!" the attacker said. "Goddamnit! Really? You had to bite me?"

"I will tell you nothing," said Ramin. "I will never talk. I will never betray my brothers. I will never betray Tanya!"

"Shut up, goddammit. And calm down. It's me." Cowboy pulled off his mask. He looked around, irritated that he might get caught.

"Cowboy?" Ramin asked.

"Yeah, goddamnit."

"I thought you were going to kill me."

"Dude, if I wanted to kill ya, I'd'a done that shit ages ago," said Cowboy. "I just want to talk to you, dude. If you'll just calm the hell down."

Ramin calmed. Cowboy picked up his cowboy hat. He slid down the wall next to Ramin and chuckled. "You thought I was going to kill you, and first thing you say is you ain't going to betray Tanya? Man, you fell deep."

"My love is powerful. I do not hide that fact," Ramin said.

"Well, that's kinda what I was lookin' to talk to ya about, if it's all the same."

"Tanya?" Ramin said, suddenly agitated. "You cannot have her. She is mine. My great love."

"No, gawd, no! Not Tanya," said Cowboy. "No offense, buddy, but she ain't exactly my brand of hooch. What I want to talk about is like, how you feel about her."

"You want me to talk about how I feel about Tanya?"

"More like that feeling, in general—that lovey-dovey feeling. Kind of gay but totally not gay, if you catch my drift? I've been having these kinds of feelings I ain't never had before for my girl Clora, see? And it's messing with my head. I don't even like it when other girls look at her, let alone that slick bastard Joaquim. I want her to be my mine, you know? Not my property—I ain't that old-fashioned, though I don't see what's so wrong with that..."

"You have fallen hard too," said Ramin.

"S'ppose," admitted Cowboy. "Problem is, I don't know how to say what I feel for her. It all comes out club-footed. And seeing as you're some kind of poet..."

"I write."

"Well, maybe you could help me express myself like that— with a little wordplay razzle dazzle."

"You want me to write you a poem for Clora?"

"Hell no. This ain't no Cyrano DeBergerac," said Cowboy, impressing himself with the reference. "Naw, just instruct me on how to do it." Ramin looked skeptical, so Cowboy got real. "I need your help, man. Didn't nobody help you with getting Tanya?"

Ramin thought about Ruti's pep talk, and he had to admit it had given him great strength and confidence. Ramin took a deep breath. He thought about all that he still longed to share with Tanya. He felt a glimmer of inspiration. "Start simply," Ramin said. "What is it about her that inspires you, specifically?"

"Dumb question," said Cowboy. "Have you seen her in a bikini?"

"You admire her body," Ramin found himself saying. "That's a start. What else?"

"Well, I guess, I can see my future with her body. Like anything's possible with her body. And I can make my dreams happen... with her body."

Less eloquently put, but it was precisely how Tanya made Ramin feel, if he was honest.

With Tanya, he would become the great poet he longed to be—universally admired and generously compensated. He could see her in the audience watching him receive his first award. He could see her on his arm at cocktail receptions, maybe being interviewed about his talents by gossip magazines. She would gush.

It was then that Ramin understood a universal truth about love, at least from the male perspective: Love is about finding the person with whom your dreams seem possible. A woman's affection, a woman's loyalty, and yes, a woman's body will inspire you to the greatest heights you can achieve in this short lifetime.

And it's not all selfish. Surely the world will also benefit from the fullness of that future. For Ramin, the globally-loved poet. For Cowboy, well, he could hardly imagine. And that is why people react so violently to love lost; why many take their own lives: Their lives have already been taken from them—that brilliant *future-them* has been murdered in cold blood. Sure, there are other lovers out there who might spark a vision, but none who can fulfill the dream that they are absolutely certain is their destiny.

"Write that," Ramin instructed Cowboy. "If it is the truth. About her body. And why it inspires love in your heart."

"I do love her, man," Cowboy said, desperation in his eyes. "She makes me a better man. A better chef. And no one makes me harder for longer."

"Refocus," Ramin cut in. "Stick with the feeling. Poetry is about metaphor. If you like her body, have it represent something beautiful in nature. Like the mountains of Quijiqua."

"Whoa! I ain't getting into all that Arab nonsense," said Cowboy. "How about a saddle?"

"Excuse me?"

"Like a soft leather saddle on a steed—on a dewy morning—ready to ride that baby into the hills, you know?"

"You would have to tread very carefully with that one."

"I got this," Cowboy said. He hugged Ramin, close and long, shocking the poet. "Thank you, man! Thank you so very much!" Cowboy was about to stand up, but turned to Ramin again, his leathered fist scrunching Ramin's shirt: "If you tell anybody about this, I will string you up. Understand?"

"I do," said Ramin.

A big smile spread over Cowboy's face. He was manic. "Let's hope that's exactly what Clora says!"

And as Cowboy stood up and sauntered off, clicking his heels in joy, Ramin spoke his first words ever in Yiddish: *"Oy gavalt,"* he said.

Tanya, he supposed, would be delighted.

Even potentially career-ending blackmail could not get in the way of Genevieve Jennings' morning beauty protocol. She bathed luxuriously in Ahava sea salt, deep conditioned her hair, and took an hour to pick out just the right silk blouse and tight black pants to center her outfit. Her lipstick was MAC's "Mellow Rage Red," and her eyes were shaded a fierce emerald. The sea air had done wonders for her skin.

She looked like dynamite. Unconquerable, just as she had

been in college, as Vice-President of her Sigma Tau Epsilon chapter. Even after that dumb bitch leaked an email where she berated a sorority sister for not fucking enough Delta Phi dudes and it went viral (a well-written email that was totally on point but derided because everyone was jealous of her), Genevieve was still a Big Woman On Campus. All she needed was a quick minute to get herself together mentally and the world was hers. (FYI, that chick who leaked the email was now working the Avis rental counter somewhere in San Jose). She could do this. She could do anything.

"Genevieve Mutherfucking Jennings," she said to the mirror. And she liked the way her voice sounded. Authoritative. Sharp.

The drive over to Eilat's Central Bank was silent. Sara and Al-Asari were on edge, scanning for police, but Jennings was completely at ease. She looked out the window at the sleepy streets of downtown Eilat and smiled. Quaint little town. Adorable. Even the dirty stray dogs and fat old men pushing falafel carts down the block were charming, and... *holy shit! Is that an Anthropologie outlet in that mini-mall?* She'd have to come back.

Yes, everything was going Jennings' way again. She would just get the money, erase the incriminating sexts between her and her boss, and get back on track for that promotion. In an hour, everything would be roses.

When they arrived in front of the bank, Jennings was almost giddy to get this party started. "That's it? No pep talk?" she said to Al-Asari. "No, 'If you alert the police, I'll kill your family?' I expected more from you."

"Only in the movies, my dear," Al-Asari said.

"Oh come on. At least give it a try. I want a speech."

Al-Asari sighed, turning back in his seat. "From the moment I laid eyes on you, Genevieve Jennings, I knew you had a lion's heart," he said. "Queen of the jungle. Everything is your prey. Now go inside that bank, fierce lion, flash your deadly claws, and get that money."

Jennings had to hand it to him. "That'll do," she said and exited the car. Winking at the two security guards posted at the front door, she breezed into the bank.

The place was bland even by Israeli standards—ugly Formica flooring, unflattering florescent lights, pens chained to table-tops. Reminded her of the DMV in Queens that she'd had the misfortune of visiting when she first moved to New York.

Behind plexi-glass, bored-looking tellers handed out wads of shekels and stamped documents. *Stamps!* Was this the 70s? *This will be a cinch*, she thought. Jennings waited behind a mother of three whose youngest child kept whining and yanking the corny velvet rope.

"*Sheket*," the mother snapped at her child.

Jennings got down on her knees and opened her purse. "Lollipop?" she said. "It's from America."

The boy smiled and took the candy. The mother smiled too, "*Bevakasha.*"

I'm an amazing person, thought Jennings.

In a moment, it was her turn. She approached the teller. "I'd like to make a withdrawal," she heard herself say, and she liked the timbre in her voice. "It's production funds for an American television production that I oversee." She handed the man her passport, along with a bank form showing the account number and the amount of funds currently in the account.

He yawned as he scanned it all. "Two million, six hundred thousand, and four shekels?" the teller said.

"Yes, but I'll take only half," said Jennings. "Let's keep that nice extra pad in the bank for a while, shall we? Want to accrue that interest."

"So one million, three hundred thousand, and two shekels," the teller said, unimpressed. "In what denomination would you like it?"

"Oh, gee, hadn't thought of that," said Jennings. "Um, hundreds?"

"Ms. Jennings, may I have a word?" a man's voice said from behind her.

Jennings momentarily lost her breath. She turned to see a short, smiling man with a horrible comb-over.

JENNINGS (INT.): "He was like Danny DeVito in *Twins*, but Israeli and without the hot brother. *Did I just date myself with that reference? Cut that or you're fired…" (*trimmed in post).

"I didn't mean to startle you," the man said. He had laugh lines across his plump face. "My name is Shlomie Shavit. I am the manager here. If you could come with me for a brief moment, please, I can get all this sorted out."

"But what about my withdrawal?" Jennings said, half turning to the teller.

"Yes, I will handle," the smiling Manager said.

Jennings looked around for Security—they didn't budge. No drama. No one seemed to suspect that a terrorist was parked just outside the bank waiting for her. But the delay *was* awkward. The teller shrugged and called for the next in line.

"Please," said the Manager, who wore a burgundy blazer.

They walked to the back of the bank and into a small, bright office with soft chairs and a bowl of hard candy on the desk. On the walls were diplomas and certificates written in Hebrew and English. There was also an elaborately framed photograph of the Manager arm-in-arm with a curvy and beautiful blonde woman, easily a foot taller than him. She wore a baking apron and held a tray of something that looked like vanilla brownies. In the photo, the Manager looked so happy, you'd have thought he'd won the lottery, and she was the prize.

Jennings took a seat. The Manager sat across from her. He said nothing. Just put on some reading glasses, eyed his computer screen, and nodded. He glanced at Jennings, then looked back at the computer screen, and sighed. Jennings knew this game. She'd been interviewed dozens of times for various big jobs with far more at stake than this. *The first fifteen seconds are key. You need to set the tone, find common ground. People who get right down to business never get what they want,* and she sensed that if she got right down to business, she wouldn't get the money.

"Your wife is a baker?" Jennings asked, motioning towards the photograph.

Her gamble was right—Shavit's face lit up, laugh lines reappearing around his eyes. "My Ruchama!" he said. "She is gifted with all baking. It doesn't help my waistline, but when she asks me to taste, how can I refuse?"

"Happy wife, happy life," Jennings said.

The banker grinned mischievously and opened his desk drawer. "You must try," he said.

He pulled out a small paper plate with a single square of pastry. "No one makes better. She is known as the Halva Queen among our friends, and has even sold some to local bakeries. Go ahead, taste."

"I couldn't take your only piece," said Jennings.

"I have gobbled six just today." The Manager laughed.

Jennings was on a strict no-carb diet, so she intended to take just a nibble, but when the melt of honey cashews hit her mouth, the flavors made her gasp, and she quickly wolfed down the rest.

"Are you kidding me with those flavors?" Jennings said, crumbs falling on her blouse. "How are you not morbidly obese? I'd do nothing else all day but consume this."

"That is great problem with my life. My wife? She caresses me with velvet, then prods me with a stick. Insists that I jog, then shows up with baked goods that could part the Red Sea."

"Rich man's problem."

"Yes." The Manager chuckled, delighted. He turned his attention back to his computer screen. "And it seems as though you have a rich woman's problem, Ms. Jennings."

"Please call me Genevieve," Jennings smiled. "After that pastry, we're on a first-name basis."

"Well, Genevieve, I see that you make a living in television, so you work in narratives. Maybe explain this narrative for me. A lovely woman walks into a bank from a foreign country and requests the withdrawal of a large sum of cash on short notice. This has red flags all over it."

"I was informed that it was all arranged well in advance," said Jennings.

"It was. Sort of. You were to arrive with a co-signee," Shavit said.

"Warren Lopez?" said Jennings. "Oh, he's sick. Bad hummus."

"Shame," the Manager said. "So tell me, if not with Mr. Lopez, how did you arrive today?"

"I was driven," said Jennings.

The Manager tilted his computer screen—there was a live feed of Sara's car parked in the security cam, Al-Asari in full view.

"This is your ride?" he said.

"My producers," Jennings said. "That's Sara Sinek, and that's..."

"Why did they not come in with you?"

"Parking," said Jennings. "I told them to wait since this should only take a moment."

"Well, I am sorry, Ms. Jennings... Genevieve. I am afraid there will be some waiting time. I am not permitted to release the funds today. Even if Mr. Lopez were here, it would take several days to process."

"But your bank assured us it would be okay if we faxed you his signature. Did you not receive the fax?"

"Yes, I received it. And a call, too. Unusual that an American television producer named Lopez would have an Arabic accent."

"He's an odd guy," said Jennings.

"A five-day waiting period is policy under such circumstances. Apologies, but my hands are tied in this matter," the Manager said. He folded his fingers over his stomach, leaned back in his chair, and shrugged.

Jennings had been in this situation before too. And while to others it would have been the end of the road, she had been on the receiving end of many no's in her life and knew them to be only a gateway to yes. "I completely understand," smiled Jennings. "It's irregular. You have your rules to follow. You simply cannot do it."

"Thank you for understanding," said the Manager. "When you come back next week with Mr. Lopez, I will bring even more halva."

"The withdrawal *is* a bit suspect," Jennings cut in. "And if a problem arose in the future, it would come down on your head. Smart move to be cautious."

"So we are agreed," he said, buoyant. "Perhaps I can speed it up to three days if we keep in touch." The Manager made a move to stand up.

"Such a shame, though," Jennings said, licking her fingers of halva crumbs. "I mean, what with your wife's delicious baking. We are looking for a local judge to use in our filming today. Someone of your wife's talent would have been perfect for the show. She could probably teach our chefs a thing or two. But with production shut down due to lack of funds, I'm afraid this opportunity would have to pass her by. Do you think she'll be disappointed?"

The Manager blanched.

"Ah, she probably doesn't want to be on TV anyway," Jennings said with a chuckle.

The Manager emitted a chuckle too, but his was nervous and tight. "Well, she wouldn't rule it out..."

"Then what a real shame. Our *Nervous Bakedown* challenge today features halva, and that will have to be thrown out the window."

"But halva is her best dish!" the Manager said, exasperated. Sweat beaded on his forehead. "You have just tasted it. She is known to all our neighbors."

"Such a shame," said Jennings, thinking hard. "She would have really gotten along with Philippe, I can tell."

"Philippe... Do you mean Philippe Duval?" The Manager was incredulous. "He is here in Eilat? My Ruchama would sit with Philippe Duval?"

"Well, not anymore," said Jennings. She got up from her chair. "Anyway, thanks so much for your help, Mr. Shavit. Need to let the crew know we're on hiatus. And good luck to your wife. Hard for someone to make it these days without TV exposure, but she's got the talent, so I'm certain that everything will work out for the both of you."

"Wait!" The banker nearly leapt over his desk. He wiped the sweat from his forehead with a small, folded handkerchief. "Perhaps I can speak to my Regional Manager. There is such a thing as emergency funds, you see, and if I personally oversee it, I would just have to bring the funds to the set and have Mr. Lopez co-sign before the money is released. You say that my wife would shoot with Philippe Duvall today?"

"In just a few short hours," said Jennings. "Do you really think she'll go for it?"

JENNINGS (INT.) (winks to camera): **"Gruesome, isn't it?"**

Out in front of the bank, Sara and Al-Asari sat listening to police radio for any sign that things had gone awry. The two guards at the door hadn't moved in minutes, even to adjust their walkies, so that was a good sign.

"This is taking longer than it should," Al-Asari said.

"Patience," Sara said, "She just got in there."

Sara's cellphone rang—the main office from the resort. "Yup?"

"Turn on the news," said Ruti. "Do it now."

Sara flipped the dial from police radio to local news and heard the following report: "...Police evidence suggests that the terrorist attack perpetrated last week in Haifa was the work of Hezbollah and not Mal-Malaika as previously reported. Hezbollah has taken full responsibility for the attack, and several suspects are in police custody. Mal-Malaika are no longer connected to the bombing but still wanted for questioning."

Sara pulled out a pack of cigarettes and offerred it to Al-Asari. Al-Asari plucked out a cigarette but just held it in his hands. Sara thought he might cry from relief.

"You're supposed to smile," Sara said. "You can go home now. You and your men are free."

"Free?" Al-Asari frowned. He snapped out of his daze and placed the cigarette in his mouth. "Ten years gone from military service and you have become naïve?"

"But they just said..."

"That we are wanted for questioning. Do you not recall what that means?" said Al-Asari. "They will have us in cells for months, and force us to confess to who knows what other crimes to keep us longer. We are still marked men."

"They can't do that now," Sara said. "It's public record that you are innocent."

"We are criminals by virtue of being Arabs," Al-Asari said. "Even if we are not in jail, our rights will be further infringed. We will be subjected to a curfew, and barred from travel. How can we support our families without crossing the border to work? No, there is no going back. Not ever. We must go on with the plan. Or we must die."

A knock came on the car door and both Sara and Al-Asari flinched. Jennings stood there next to a short man in a burgundy jacket and a comb-over. He appeared almost grotesquely happy, laugh lines spread all over his face. He carried a large metal briefcase handcuffed to his wrist.

"My producers," said Jennings, as the Manager slid into the backseat with her. He smiled and nodded enthusiastically. "Sara, one stop before we head back to the resort. We found a local judge for today's baking challenge. Mr. Shavit's wife is a halva legend."

"She's amazing, I assure you," the Manager said, elated by the turn of events. "Best halva in the Middle East!"

They drove through the streets of Eilat. The Manager gave directions, breathless with excitement. When they arrived on his block of small, semi-detached houses, he could not contain himself. "You must come in. All of you, please!"

Sara, Jennings, and Al-Asari followed the man to the front door of his home. When he opened the door, a wave of caramel and butter wafted into every nostril. Sara drooled on her chin.

"Ruchama? We have company, my dear," the Manager said.

"Not now, Shlumie. I am baking," a woman's voice said from the next room.

"Ruchama, very important company," the Manager sang.

"Can't it wait? I will ruin the whole batch," the woman said.

Soon she appeared; tall, blonde, and curvy, patting flour off of her fingers and onto her baking apron.

"Wow," said Jennings.

Ruchama was even more gorgeous in person—bright green eyes and wavy hair. A true bombshell, an Israeli Giada De Laurentis. The Manager couldn't have been more proud.

"This is my Ruchama," he gushed, presenting her as if she was a work of art.

"A sincere pleasure," said Jennings. "Your husband allowed me a taste of your pastry. You have a rare culinary gift."

"Ach, that batch is two days old!" she said, embarrassed. "Shlumie, how could you? Come, taste this instead." Ruchama disappeared into the kitchen, then returned with a tray of warm Moroccan date cookies. In seconds, the tray was crumbs.

"How would you like to be on television?" Sara asked.

"Today," said her husband.

"Television? But I am covered in flour," said Ruchama.

"Philippe must meet you," said Jennings.

"Philippe Duval," the Manager emphasized to his wife. "You will judge next to Philippe Duvall!"

Ruchama's mouth dropped open. "B-b-but I am covered in flour," she said.

In minutes, they were all back in the car—Sara, Al-Asari, Jennings, the Bank Manager with his metal briefcase handcuffed to his wrist, and his gorgeous wife, Ruchama.

"Now everyone will know," the Manager marveled, squeezing his wife's hand. "The whole world will know of my Ruchama!"

Back at the resort, Jennings hopped onto the landline to talk to New York.

"I'm telling you, Glen, halva is the new cupcakes. We'll be way ahead of the curve on this. Think about it: The Network predicts major food trend in riveting Season Five finale. It's organic and dramatic, and we have a gorgeous local talent to judge. Who?... We discovered her... She's a knockout, like a young Cat Cora, but straight and Israeli. This will represent the coming together of the tribes. What do Jews and Arabs love more than killing each other? Halva. I'm telling you, it writes itself..."

"She's good," Al-Asari said.

"Best there is," Sara replied.

"He went for it," Jennings said after hanging up. "Now what?"

Sara shrugged. "I guess it's cameras up for *Nervous Bake-down.*"

CHAPTER 14

Two cooking stations were set up on a grassy area near the hotel pool. Beside them were two fully loaded pantries, two identical stainless-steel fridges, and one circular table covered mysteriously with a burgundy tablecloth. The original cast of *Natural Dish-aster: Season Five* gathered at their cooking station taking educated guesses.

"Probably another goddamn matzah challenge," said Etienne.

"I bet it's a whole pig that we somehow have to cook kosher," said Chef Nisha.

"Not sure that's even remotely possible," said Tanya.

"Exactly why it's probably the challenge," said Nisha.

Philippe Duvall took a seat next to the supermodel Bilha Tekeli and adjusted his purple cravat. Next to them sat the bank manager's wife, the "Halva Queen of Eilat," Ruchama Shavit. She squealed when she first met the two celebrity foodies with whom she would judge.

"I have a shrine to each one of you in my home," Ruchama had gushed. "Mr. Duvall, I highlighted so many pages of your *Restauran-tour* series that it's painted yellow. And Ms. Tekeli, if it weren't for your work with the orphaned animal shelter, I would never have found my cat Norman. He was seconds from being put down, but why put a blind two-legged cat down if he is full of love? He is in my heart even now and I thank you. You have both changed my life immeasurably and I am not worthy of sitting next to you at this table."

Tekeli shot Duvall a look. Both of them loved this poor creature on sight.

"Nonsense!" said Duvall. "It is we who are honored. We tasted your halva—from heaven itself."

"I could not stop eating," Tekeli said. "Thank God I don't do nudes anymore. You have expanded my ass immeasurably!"

"I am almost faint. You tasted my halva?" Ruchama said. "I am beyond honored."

"Tell me, Ruchama," Duvall said. "Would you like to be a bit naughty and share a cigarette with us—a three-way?"

"It would be a dream," she said.

In seconds, they were all laughing and smoking together, complaining about that sly fox Sara and calling the competition "a sham, but you know that the exposure is unmatched..."

The terrorist contestants arrived and were staged in a neat semi-circle next to their opponents. The sun was high in the sky and the sea was calm—perfect for a shoot. Sara, Ruti, and Al-Asari took their seats in the control room tent. The Bank Manager sat on a chair in the back, resting his wrist with the metal briefcase on his lap.

"Cameras up. Let's do this," Sara said into her walkie.

CJ Bazemore, in an aquamarine silk chef coat with diamond-encrusted waves across the back, settled on his mark. "Chef Cowboy, Chef Salid, your teams have chosen you to represent them in the elimination round," he said. "Sadly, one of you will be going home."

Cameras cut to sad looks from Clora, who would either play Cowboy's great love or his great betrayer (Post wasn't certain which yet, and it depended on whether she hooked up with Joaquim on camera after eliminations). Regardless, a close-up of her was crucial.

"The elimination challenge is a little game I like to call *Nervous Bakedown*," said Bazemore. "And today you will be making a favorite of this region: halva."

"Yes!" Cowboy said, high-fiving his teammates. "I'm fuckin' winning this!"

CHEF COWBOY (INT.): "Never made halva in my life. Don't even know what the hell it is. Just acted cocky to psyche out Osama over there."

"Here's how the game works," CJ Bazemore said. "Each of you will be given the very basics for Israeli halva: honey, tahini, and pistachios. To make halva, you will need only these things. But this is *Nervous Bakedown*."

With a grand flourish, Bazemore pulled the burgundy tablecloth off the round table to reveal a spinnable wheel split into eight separate sections. In all but two sections was an ingredient that would make any baked good nearly inedible: Dill pickles. Blue cheese. Salmon roe. Anchovies. Turkey jerky. And of course that old stinky favorite, durian. Two sections were left empty.

"You must spin this table of ingredients three times," said Bazemore. "If you spin the wheel and land on a blank, you are safe, but if you land on a space with an ingredient, then you must incorporate that ingredient into your halva."

CHEF JOAQUIM (INT.): "If Cowboy gets even one of those ingredients, he's boned. Imagine anchovy halva. I'm gonna have sweet Clora all to myself."

"Chef Cowboy, since you are not a murderer of innocent women and children, you have the choice—you may spin first or pass to your terrorist foe," said Bazemore.

"I'll spin," Cowboy said, and again gave his teammates high-fives.

CHEF COWBOY (INT.): "Shitting a ton o' bricks over here."

Cowboy approached the table, took a deep breath, and spun the wheel. It went around several times and then slowed. Cowboy turned pale as it settled on the salmon roe. But then, at the last millisecond, it clicked, passing into a bare spot.

"Yee-haw!" Cowboy hooted, waving around his cowboy hat.

"All clear for Chef Dex's first spin," said CJ Bazemore. "Salid, you're up,"

Salid stepped forward and grabbed the wheel. He spun, then shut his eyes. When he heard the wheel come to a stop, his team sighed while the others celebrated.

"Ouch," said Bazemore. "Unfortunately, Chef Salid, you must now incorporate blue cheese into your halva. Back to you, Cowboy."

Cowboy spun again. The table almost toppled over and it took half a minute for the wheel to finally settle. When it did...

"Yee-ha! Now that's how we do it in Texas!" Cowboy said, riding an invisible bronco. His team went mad.

"Wow," CJ Bazemore said. "Two empty spins. Only one more spin for you, Chef Dex, and no adds. Salid, you have blue cheese and two more spins."

Salid looked back at his group. Sheik was disgusted. He pounded his fist into his hand as if to say, "Win this or die." Salid didn't need any more motivation.

"Aw shiiiiit!" Cowboy called out. "Armageddon!"

And it was. Salid's spin had stopped on anchovies. His head hung low, he took the ingredient and placed it on his cooking station next to the blue cheese.

"Honestly, I have no idea how you're going to do it," said Bazemore. "Chef Dex, final spin. And in this final spin, you do have an option. You are allowed to skip your spin and choose the ingredients you want, or risk it, and place your spin in the hands of God."

Cowboy had watched enough reality TV to see an opportunity to milk screen time. He stood on his toes peering at the wheel of ingredients: dill pickles, salmon roe, durian. *Oh hell!* He turned to his teammates as if he was unsure.

"Spin it," they pleaded, especially Joaquim.

Cowboy took a deep breath. "I'll take the turkey jerky," he said.

CHEF COWBOY (INT.): "Ain't nothin' a cowboy can't do with jerky!"

"Chef Dex, you've got that turkey jerky. Now it's up to your opponent. Chef Salid, want to hand pick your ingredient or spin?"

Salid looked at Sheik, who snarled at him. Salid was sick of taking his aggressive bullshit. He spat at the ground and walked up to the table.

"Durian?!" CJ Bazemore gasped. "You must be insane!"

The cast members rejoiced. The terrorists were enraged.

Sheik dragged his thumb across his throat.

TERRORIST #7 (INT.): "Choosing durian in a halva challenge is the culinary equivalent of your suicide vest failing to ignite while in police custody. *I'm not saying this. It's crazy..." (*trimmed in post).

"Let me survey the damage here," said Bazemore. "Chef Dex, you've got turkey jerky. Chef Salid, you must incorporate blue cheese, anchovies, and durian into your halva. Tell me, Chef Salid, what are you going to do with those ingredients?"

"I will pray," Salid said.

"Well, hopefully, your team can help you out too, because you have five minutes to plan your recipe, and then only twenty minutes to create your halva. Clock starts now!"

Cowboy ran back to his team. They all gave him encouraging pats on the back. When Cowboy hugged Clora, Joaquim rolled his eyes. The team came together and explained to Cowboy how to make a simple halva.

"Don't get fancy," Clora suggested.

"Yeah, stay pedestrian. That's your thing," added Joaquim.

Clora's chuckle made Cowboy's blood boil.

"You calling me pedestrian, fool?" said Cowboy. "I'm The Cowboy Chef and I will string you up."

"Right, the cowboy wants to string up an Indian," said Joaquim.

"You're Puerto Rican," said Cowboy.

"Like you know the difference."

"We'll see who's pedestrian," snapped Cowboy. "You watch me rip this raghead apart."

"I take offense to that," said Chrissy.

On the terrorist side, Salid sat meditating while Sheik berated him. But Salid heard none of it. He was gone again, off in his memories. Salid's mother was on her deathbed. Her iron levels were dangerously low, but she was refusing to take her medicine—said it made everything foggy. Salid's sister was getting married in only a few days, and Salid's mother said she wanted to be alert for every minute of it, even if it killed her. So Salid did what he could. He infused sugary desserts with mineral supplements—fish eggs, cheese, and even once, durian. His mother made it to the wedding, and some marveled at the color in her cheeks.

"Cooking time starts now!" Bazemore announced.

Cowboy and Salid ran to their cooking stations. Cowboy grabbed the honey, the tahini, and the pistachios—the basics. He got prepping, chopping up the pistachios, but was bothered by something. Out of the corner of his eye, he spied Clora sitting next to Joaquim. They weren't watching or helping him. Instead, they were giggling at some dumb joke, and she was touching his arm.

"Fuck that noise," Cowboy muttered to himself. "I ain't losing my girl to no reekin' Rican dude."

Cowboy dropped his work and marched back to the pantry. He made a big show of picking out additional ingredients—dark chocolate, dates, and just to prove his point, elderflower. He strutted back to his table and slammed down the ingredients, but Clora was still giggling at that assclown, not paying Cowboy a lick of attention. "Imagine, a homebred Texas girl getting dazzled by that New York slickster. Well, no siree, Bob. I ain't puttin' up with that horseshit."

Cowboy went back to the pantry again. He saw lemons, put his hand on brown sugar, and looked back—Clora still wasn't looking his way. It was time to make a statement. So he opened the fridge and got out the pork butt.

"Hey, Cowboy, what the hell are you doing?" Tanya called out.

"I'm showing you jackasses how it's done Texas style!" He fired up the grill and slapped down the meat, then muttered, "Now that ought to get her damn attention."

And it did. "You've got to admire his courage," Clora said to Joaquim, who frowned.

Cowboy grinned. "That's right! Ain't no ISIS gonna defeat a true cowboy. Yee-haw!"

"Yee-haw!" said his teammates.

Meanwhile, Salid was hard at work. He hacked the durian in half, letting the flatulent smell waft into his nostrils as he sliced it thin and laid it on the grill. He ground up the salmon roe and anchovies and added honey to soften their strong flavors. If he got it right, you'd still taste the fishy quality, but it would work as a savory balance against the cloying sweetness of the halva.

In the control room tent, Jennings hovered over Sara's shoulder. "It's all about cutaways," she said. "Get in that pot. If we don't see the process, we have no story."

"Get those cameras inside those pots," Sara walkied. "Need to see the process."

"Good. What about the teams. How are they reacting?" Jennings said.

"Camera four's on wide. We'll do reactions in pick-ups and

spray the whole thing down."

"No, I want organic, in-the-moment reactions," said Jennings. "What's Clora doing? Cowboy is clearly showing off for her."

"You think?" Sara said. "Camera four, get in on Clora. Story there." And indeed Clora was blowing kisses to Cowboy while Joaquim sulked in the background.

"Nice catch," Sara said to Jennings.

Jennings smiled. She felt good. Everything was at it should be. The contest was coming off with nice drama, and the food might even be edible.

"I've got to go ten-one," Sara said to Jennings. "How about you step in and direct for a bit?" Jennings was taken aback. "Between us producers, the camera work on *Celebrity Pre-nup* was cutting edge. Would be nice to get some of that in here," Sara added.

Jennings noticed Al-Asari watching. She grinned. "I'll give you five minutes," she said.

Jennings took the director's chair and began yammering immediately. "Get in those pots and then back up to faces. This is basic, guys. Need to see that raw emotion—pots, faces, pots, faces. Don't be shy! Get in there!" The cameras jerked back and forth, causing Jennings to have a conniption about lack of instinct. "What is this, amateur hour?" she said to the DP with a grin, but forgot to turn off her walkie, so everyone heard. Even the Bank Manager, who sat there with his briefcase cuffed to his wrist, winced at that faux pas.

Sara and Al-Asari met outside of the tent, away from the action. "I thought you said you were ready," Sara said.

"It is late, but they will be here. I have no doubt," said Al-Asari.

"Hey," Ruti cut in, "what are you two scheming about over there?" She'd been standing a few feet away. "Who will be here?"

"Oh, just the judging panel," Sara said. "If you can believe it, Ruchama has become a prima donna already."

"I don't believe it," Ruti said. She turned to Al-Asari. "How's your hand?"

"Healing up nicely. Thank you again for being so gentle with me," said Al-Asari.

"Well, I needed you alive... for now," Ruti said, without a lick of sarcasm.

"Medic!" a producer called out. "Cowboy's cut."

"Gotta go," Ruti said. "Stop scheming, you two. You look suspicious." Then she ran off with her first-aid kit.

"Make sure the cast is put on ice," Jennings barked into the walkie when they announced a TV timeout. "Does this thing work?" She glared at her walkie. "It's like they don't even hear me."

"Let me swap the battery and do a walkie check," said an over-eager Production Assistant. He handed Jennings a new one.

"Thank God," she said, then spoke into her new walkie: "I said, 'Put those cast members on ice! They're goofing around.' Then again, that could be a story."

But the cast wouldn't stop talking, and there was nothing any producer could do. Ramin had passed Tanya a note, which Chef LizZ intercepted: "A thousand moons do not capture your brightness," LizZ read aloud. "Ha! What is this? Jihadist propaganda?"

"Give me that!" Tanya said. "It's sweet."

"Tanya's banging Salman Rushdie," said Etienne.

"We're back on the clock. Continue to cook," said CJ Bazemore, and the cast resumed cheering on Cowboy.

Soon, both Salid and Cowboy had their halva in the oven. With a minute left, CJ Bazemore took center stage to count it down, this time in Hebrew. "And that's time! Hands off your food!" Salid and Cowboy raised their hands burglar-style. "Cowboy, time to present your dish to the judges," said Bazemore.

At the judges' table, Ruchama whispered a joke into Bilha's ear and the supermodel exploded in laughter.

"Hey, no secrets! We're a team," chided Duvall. "You two are so naughty together. I love it."

Sara walked over to settle them down. "Remember, this is the big moment—huge stakes. Both chefs are terrified of your opinion. So act the part, please."

As Sara walked away, Ruchama mimicked Sara's overly serious demeanor, and Duvall and Bilha cracked ribs laughing.

Cowboy approached the judges' table, plates in hand. "Well, hello there, y'all. My name is Chef Cowboy and I decided to step out of my comfort zone a bit on this. You see, I'm from West Texas, and there ain't almost nothin' we do with food out there that ain't got barbeque. So what I've created is a savory pork butt and turkey jerky halva with pistachios and honey. You enjoy now, ya hear?"

The three judges took bites, closing their eyes to deconstruct the flavors. Cowboy was delighted to see the Halva Queen take a second bite. Sara intended for Philippe Duvall to speak first, then Bilha, then the newly minted Halva Queen, but Ruchama broke in first.

"I've been to Texas," Ruchama said, "and this really tells me who you are, and I appreciate that. It's an unorthodox choice— creative. Cowboy, your halva, like you, has guts to spare."

"Well, I sure do appreciate that, ma'am," Cowboy said, bowing.

"The texture suffered a bit," Ruchama continued, "and the paste was a bit over-cooked and crumbly. I like my halva with a silky texture. Plus, authentic West Texas barbeque has a mesquite wood flavor that I so adore. I'm missing that bitter taste that would have paired so well with the pistachios. But overall an impressive dish."

It was a solid critique. Sara cued Bilha, but the Halva Queen had covered all of her points, so she went to her fallback, which she knew would make the cut.

"This felt big and hot in the mouth," said the supermodel. "My tongue experienced a gooey explosion of flavor that had me craving more."

"Bravo, young chap!" Philippe Duvall said next. "I'm afraid I may have underestimated the breadth of your talent. What you have created here is something innovative—good savory-to-sweet flavors. Nice balance with the dates. I am far from halva royalty, but I must admit that I do like a little crumble in my halva. So I give full points, save for plating, which could have been tidier."

Cowboy turned to his teammates. "You hear that, baby?" he said, looking to Clora. "Duvall said he underestimated the breath of my talent."

"*Breadth*," Joaquin corrected him.

"Whatever," Cowboy said. He then turned to the camera operators. "Hey, camera ops: Follow my lead. I got somethin' to say."

In the control tent, Jennings practically hopped out of her skin. "We've got a runner! Get on him. I need cutaways to Clora and Joaquin, stat. Do it now. Something big is happening. I feel it in my bones."

Cowboy walked up to Clora. He pulled a crinkled piece of paper from his pocket and took her hand. He waited for full camera coverage before he spoke, but he was beaming.

"My love for you is like a saddle," Cowboy read, "soft and firm on assless chaps…" Clora looked back at him confused, and Cowboy saw one of the camera guys crack up. He balled up the paper and tossed it over his shoulder. "Darlin', I was gonna wait to do this, but my Grandpa Buck always said there ain't no damn time like the present."

Cowboy got down on one knee and took off his cowboy hat. Inside the hat was a little velvet box.

"We've got a marriage proposal! I don't believe it!" Jennings cried out. "Coverage! Coverage! Leave the judges! Holy shit, the ratings are going to go through the roof!"

"Now, baby, we been goin' hot 'n heavy for some time now," said Cowboy. "And, well, I just can't quit you—not in a gay way. No offense, Chef LizZ."

"None taken," she said, her smiling eyes already wet.

Clora gasped as Cowboy opened the velvet box, revealing an impressively sparkly diamond ring. Tears streamed down her face.

"Clora, I told you when we met, I never known any girl like you," said Cowboy. "You elevate me as a man. You give me a breath of talent. So whaddya say, girl? Will you marry me?"

Clora shrieked and collapsed into Cowboy's arms. "Yes!" she said.

"Yes!" Jennings celebrated in the control room. "I called it! Didn't I call it, Sara? Admit I called it!"

"You called it," said Sara, just then walking back into the tent with Al-Asari.

"In Post, we're going to have to put Salid's judging prior to Cowboy—we need to end with this gold," said Jennings, tearing up. "What an act-out! *Oh my God!*"

"Copy that," said Sara.

"Holy shit! A spontaneous proposal," Jennings continued. "I am so getting that promotion. I can't wait to text Glen."

Everyone cheered the newly engaged couple. Nisha squeezed Ghana's hand and smiled. Even the terrorists clapped—they didn't want to seem callous.

TERRORIST #7 (INT.): "When I took my fourth bride, it was romantic like this…. *this is offensive. I refuse to say such a thing!" (*trimmed in post).

TANYA (INT.): "Gotta hand it to Cowboy. Not a dry panty in the house."

Once things settled down, there was still TV business to attend to. Bazemore dabbed at tears on the collar of his silk chef coat. "Didn't see that coming," Bazemore said. "And I know you two lovebirds are eager to consummate this proposal, but we still have to judge Chef Salid's dish."

After some repositioning that would allow the editors to cut it both ways, and a ton of Kleenex for Team Mise En Bouche, Salid stepped to the judges' table. He laid down three plates of halva, and the mere aroma had the judges in a state of dizziness. As Salid stood back in position, he even let out a proud chuckle. He knew, after all, that what he had served on those plates was a culinary masterpiece, a halva so succulent, innovative, and strange that it would have major reverberations in the culinary world-at-large for years to come.

There would be a total rethink on how chefs use pistachios, and a new global food trend that would spur multi-million dollar industries, cause food empires to rise, and have families fighting over the sweet crumbs of success.

Salid knew his creation was heavenly, so he was looking forward to the judges showering praise on him.

Then a far-off hum was heard in the sky. "Hold for audio," said the 2nd AD.

All crew waited for the noise to pass, but the hum grew to a rumble. The judges were all salivating over their plates but still unable to eat.

"What is that annoyance?" Jennings said.

"Sounds like a fleet of lawnmowers," Sara said.

"It's happening," Al-Asari whispered to Sara. "Right now."

"I think it's a helicopter," Chef Nisha said.

"That or a stampede," said Cowboy.

The chefs and terrorists felt the earth vibrate beneath their feet. "Does Israel have earthquakes?" asked Chrissy.

"That ain't no earthquake," Joaquim said. He pointed off into the distance, where a great cloud of dust whirled in the air.

And in the midst of it... "Are those camels?"

"You've got to be shitting me," said Cowboy.

Dozens of camels raced toward the set, their hooves kicking up a cloud of dust and creating a great cacophony of rhythmic clops. Heavily bearded men in Bedouin garb rode in, waving curved swords in the air. At the front of the herd was a man with a wispy beard and wearing vintage, white-framed Ray-Bans.

"Rashik-ang!" Strider, the absentee director of *Natural Dishaster: Season Five*, pointed his sword towards the set, and the Bedouin Camel Warriors followed his orders.

"Who the hell is that?" Jennings said. "What the hell is going on?!"

"It's Strider," said Sara. "Our Lead Director."

"I thought you said he was sick."

"Lopez had him shooting a sizzle for Nomad Network about Bedouin Camel Warriors. I guess he's back."

"You lied to me," Jennings said.

"I-I..."

"Well, he's not getting his seat back," Jennings proclaimed. "I called that marriage proposal. I earned the damn seat. You tell him that, okay?"

"Will do."

The Bedouins, swords drawn, surrounded the set. Sara looked to Al-Asari for an explanation, but he had left the tent. Suddenly, the terrorists, including Salid, all took off running from the set towards the resort. Sara spotted Al-Asari among them.

"What the fuck are they doing?" Sara said and ran out of the control room to follow.

The terrorists entered the main resort and then, seconds later, came out of a different exit.

They looked disoriented, but Al-Asari pointed the way to the docks. "Go now!" he yelled.

And that was when another loud noise erupted and the source quickly became known. A large black military helicopter swooped down towards the beach, passing right above the great rush of men on camels. As the helicopter angled itself towards the ground next to the docks, the terrorists went rushing towards it. Al-Asari peeled off from the men and ran back into the control room tent. This time he had a gun. Jennings and the rest of the crew put up their hands. Al-Asari pointed his gun at the Bank Manager.

"Hand over the briefcase," Al-Asari said.

"But I'm cuffed," said the Manager, trembling with fear.

Al-Asari pushed the barrel of the gun to the banker's wrist.

He tightened the length of chain and shot through it.

When Ruchama heard the gunfire and saw Al-Asari run out of the control room tent with her husband's briefcase, she collapsed in tears.

"They killed my husband!" she cried.

Al-Asari ran off towards the docks. The helicopter was just settling onto the ground and the terrorists gathering in a clump to board it. But when the pilot saw a herd of camels ridden by Bedouin Warriors stampeding towards him, he reared the helicopter back off the ground.

"We are destroyed!" Al-Asari screamed.

But just as the camels neared the beach, they were cut off. A custom van with a naked woman riding a unicorn spray-painted on the hood screeched out in front, causing the camels to stop in their tracks and to rear back in fear and confusion. The van skidded to a stop and the side door flung open. Out emerged Warren Lopez and his wife Sharon, who pointed a semi-automatic machine gun towards the helicopter.

"This is for fucking with a pregnant woman!" she screamed, opening fire.

But just as the first few bullets left the chamber, both Sharon and Warren were tackled by what felt like a Mack truck. They fell onto the ground with a thud. CJ Bazemore held them down.

"Stay down, you idiots," Bazemore said, his voice suddenly suggesting a low and scratchy Israeli accent.

"Hey! What'd you do that for?" said Warren.

"I said, 'Shut up!'" said CJ Bazemore. "You'll ruin everything."

"But I almost killed the terrorists," said Sharon.

"We've been hunting those bastards for years," said Bazemore. "If we kill them now, we'll never find their base."

"Who are you?" asked Sharon.

"Mossad," said Bazemore.

"CJ Bazemore is an Israeli spy," Warren said. "Now ain't that a son of a bitch?"

"I said to shut up!" Bazemore hurled the couple back into the van like a couple of potato sacks and jumped into the driver's seat. He plunged an enormous cigar into his mouth, lit it, and pressed on the pedal. "Fucking Americans," he said gruffly, driving off.

With the camels too spooked to be controlled, the helicopter found its footing again by the dock and landed. Sara ran back to the control room, where she found Jennings still directing cameras, and the Bank Manager on the ground, pale-faced and sweating, rubbing his bare wrist.

"Where's the briefcase?" Sara said.

"He nearly killed me," the Manager said.

"Where's Al-Asari?"

"How would I know?" cried the Manager. "Don't let him get away with my money!"

Sara rushed out of the control room and took off towards the docks.

Al-Asari boarded the helicopter, briefcase in hand. The terrorists lined up to follow him, but Al-Asari gave the pilot the signal to take off. When one terrorist put a hand on the deck to pull himself up, Al-Asari pointed his gun at the man's head. The terrorist backed away and, as he did, noticed the bullet holes from Sharon Lopez's gun, which had punctured the helicopter's gas tank. Gasoline was spilling out from a thick black hole. The terrorist pointed to the hazard and began to sprint away in fear.

The helicopter hovered above ground and Al-Asari settled into his seat as Sara ran up to the dock and tried to hurl herself onboard. As the helicopter teetered from her weight, Al-Asari's gun slid on the floor and fell out the side of the helicopter and into the water below.

Sara pulled herself off the ground and into the copter as it took flight. Immediately, she lunged for the briefcase. Al-Asari fought her for it, smashing the case against Sara's face. The helicopter reared up and sent them both tumbling to the floor. Sara slammed Al-Asari in the chin and got a hold of his leg to bite, but Al-Asari gave a kick that sent Sara onto her back.

"Son of a bitch, I'll kill you!" Sara screamed.

The briefcase slid along the floor and almost fell out of the helicopter as they pummeled each other mercilessly. Onlookers from below saw a great fistfight in the sky, the helicopter tilting as each fighter landed lethal blows.

"They're going to kill each other," Jennings said over walkie. "Get as tight as you can on their faces. I want to see raw emotion."

But when the helicopter got high enough that it was out of range for the cameras, the fighting stopped abruptly. Sara and Al-Asari collapsed onto the floor next to each other, gasping for breath.

"You didn't have to punch me so hard in the nose," said Al-Asari.

"We needed them to believe," said Sara, wincing as she touched her bruised jaw.

Sara sat up and pulled out a duffle bag from under the passenger's seat. Inside were two large rubber sacks packed with wet suits, flippers, and scuba tanks. Sara passed Al-Asari his rubber sack, but then positioned the briefcase between them.

"You do the honors," Al-Asari said.

"No, you. I insist," said Sara.

Al-Asari grinned. He clicked open the briefcase. "To a new life," he said.

"To freedom," said Sara.

The case opened wide. It was packed with money. Al-Asari reached in and threw a stack into his bag. Sara did the same but, when she lifted the middle stack, she felt a hard edge at the bottom of the case. It felt like velcro. She pulled it back.

In the middle of the bundle was a digital clock with explosives rigged to red and blue wires. The clock read "four seconds." Sara looked at Al-Asari. "Three." Al-Asari scrambled to his feet. "Two." Sara grabbed the briefcase, flinging it towards the door. "One." And as it sailed out towards the open air, Sara thought about Nathan and how she would do anything at that moment to be back with him singing some horrible Adele song at home. "Zero."

Onlookers witnessed a great explosion in the sky.

A massive orange flame suspended there for several seconds, then crashed into the waves of the Red Sea.

Swimmers rushed out of the water. Sirens blared.

In the control room tent, there was a sense of awe—the DP rubbed his eyes, not quite believing what he'd just witnessed.

"Aw shit," Jennings said. "Tell me we got that on camera?"

"Got it, boss," said the DP, and they high-fived.

Military police crashed down the gates of the Grand Sheba Excelsior and rushed onto the resort grounds. Men in bulletproof vests pointed guns at anything that moved. The Cravat and the Supermodel huddled, terrified. The Halva Queen lay next to her husband inside the control room tent.

"I love you so much, Shlumie," she cried. "I thought you were gone."

By the docks, the terrorists were face down, cuffed around their wrists and ankles. IDF soldiers screamed and kicked them in the ribs. When the soldiers began to remove the terrorists' masks, they were surprised to find that each terrorist had duct tape covering his mouth. The terrorists' petrified eyes bugged out as they pleaded in muffled tones. One soldier peeled the duct tape off a terrorist's mouth. "They swapped us!" the terrorist screamed. "We are chefs, not terrorists. Swear to God! Don't shoot!"

As duct tape was removed from the other terrorists, all screamed the same story. The police searched the beach for any other terrorists who might have gotten away. They found none.

DUAL INTERVIEW: JOAQUIM & CHRISSY

CHRISSY (INT.): "When the masks came off and everyone realized these were the original fake terrorists, it was like, 'Awww shit, someone's gettin' fired.'"

JOAQUIM (INT.): "Word is Mossad still questioned the fuck out of them, to the point where one of the chefs turned and joined ISIS."

CHRISSY (INT.): "Dude, you completely made that up."

JOAQUIM (INT.): "Yeah, but how cool would that have been, right? I mean I don't have any direct sympathy for ISIS, but they need to eat. I bet they'd love to recruit a chef. Wonder what they'd pay?"

CHRISSY (INT.): "You really are an idiot, aren't you?"

Miles away, an old rusty bus was clanking its way out of downtown Eilat and towards Bethlehem. There were some families aboard, one or two businessmen, and then at the back a contingent of large women completely covered in burkas. One of the women was the size of an NFL defensive linesman.

"This had better work," Sheik growled to the others.

"It will," said Ramin. "Just stay pretty and we'll make it."

SHEIK (INT.): "I'm not going to say I enjoyed wearing a niqab. In fact, I have a newfound respect for women for wearing them. So hot in there! Still, it beat the hell out of that itchy mask. My neck still suffers from rash."

Back on the set of *Natural Dish-aster*, Tanya staggered around disoriented. "Ramin?" she cried out. "Ramin, where are you?" She pulled out his most recent poem and held it to her wet cheek.

At that very moment, a dazed-looking Chef Brandon limped onto the resort grounds and towards the set. His head was wrapped in a bandage from his epic fall during the *Cannibal Challenge*.

"Who's that guy?" Jennings said. "In Camera C."

"Chef Brandon. The terrorists must have released him before they left," said the DP.

"Follow him," Jennings said.

Brandon spotted Tanya wandering the set, rubbing a piece of folded paper against her cheek. He hobbled over.

"Because I like you," Brandon said to Tanya, startling her out of her reverie.

"What?" Tanya said.

"Because I really, really like you. Like a lot, Tanya," said Brandon. "That's why I cried when I came. Because I've never liked anyone quite as much before. Even my foster mother, and she was everything to me. I think I love you, Tanya."

Tanya looked at Brandon. Even with his head bandage and limp, he was quite the specimen. Sure, he was no Ramin, but Ramin was gone now. She would only have his words, and the memory of their sweet dalliance.

"Oh, Brandon," Tanya said. She fell into his muscular arms. "That's the most beautiful thing anyone's ever said to me."

The cameras caught everything. Jennings was on fire in the control room. "Don't stop shooting. Never stop shooting!" she said over walkie. "Get it all!"

The world was chaos in her quad—fire, guns, crying, kissing, screaming. Jennings loved it all. What an act-out! What a super-tease! What a season! She could write her own goddamn ticket at The Network.

Something caught her eye in Camera F, so she leaned in close to look. One of the fake terrorists, released by the police, had wandered onto the set. She watched the handsome, diminutive chef meander towards the judges' table.

"Jesus Christ, he looks like an Arabic Bobby Flay," Jennings said. "Just shorter."

The fake terrorist looked both ways to make sure no one was watching, then he grabbed a piece of the untouched halva on the judges' table and popped it in his mouth. As he savored the flavors, the chef's expression was unmistakable to Jennings: personal pride. He walked off towards the exit. Jennings rushed over, stopping him just before the gate.

"I know it's you," she said.

"*Pardonné moi?*" the man replied in French.

Jennings rolled her eyes. "You're Salid," she said. "The chef. The great chef."

"*Vous êtes confus,*" Salid said.

"I won't blow your cover," Jennings said. "Just hear me out. What if I told you that you could cook whatever you want for the rest of your life? Best ingredients available, all the staff you could ever hope for, finest kitchen—and no one will ever know who you really are?"

"*Je m'appelle Pierre,*" said Salid.

"Look, I don't care if you're the King of Denmark. You can cook, Salid, and without that ridiculous mask, you're pretty easy on the eyes too. After the storm settles here, I'm going to need another hit. And you're my hit. You. Are. My. Hit. Salid," she said. "Either that, or I turn you in." Jennings looked Salid right in the eyes. "Don't tempt a desperate woman."

Salid thought for a moment. "I never want to be anyone but me," he said.

"You have my word," Jennings said.

"No gimmicks?" Salid said.

"Just you—just Salid. Actually, not a bad title for the pilot episode," she smiled. They shook on it, then walked back to the resort together to discuss terms.

Over by the docks, the Bedouin camels were back in tight formation, pointing towards their home in Egypt.

"Hey, Strider," one of the field producers said, looking up at him on his camel. "Where you been, man?"

"Home," Strider said. "I have been home." He raised his sword to the army of the Bedouin warriors. "We ride!" he said, and the fleet of camels galloped off.

"Wait," the producer said. "I've still got your Mophie iPhone charger—the solar-powered one. I never gave it back from that shoot in Maui."

Strider looked both ways. He grabbed the charger from the producer's hand and slid it into his robe. "Thanks, dude," he said. "I'm dying to update my Instagram."

Then he rode off.

Ruti stood by the docks and gazed out at the helicopter wreckage, still aflame in the Red Sea. Her face was streaked with tears. Sara was dead. So was Al-Asari. It was all over.

She turned and walked back towards the control room tent. Inside, she found Sara's cell phone, which she'd left in the charger. There was a text from Nathan: "Call me tonight, okay?" Ruti pocketed the phone and was about to leave when the Bank Manager entered.

"My Ruti," said the Manager. "My sweetest little niece, Ruti."

"Hello, Uncle," said Ruti.

They embraced.

"Is it done?" the Bank Manager said in Ruti's ear. "Are my brother's killers finally dead?"

"Yes. Both of them," said Ruti. "You have done well, my uncle. The briefcase lit up the sky, and justice is finally served."

"I am glad," said the Manager. "Your father may not have approved of our methods, but I know he is happy in heaven. I can feel him with us."

"Me too."

A tear escaped the Manager's eye, which he wiped away. "Goodbye, my Ruti," he said. As he walked out, he pointed at a cammo backpack under his chair. "The remainder of the money. Use it well, my dear."

"Bless you, Uncle," said Ruti, and watched him walk out. Ruti pulled out Sara's cell phone and held it to her cheek.

"Goodbye, my love."

CHAPTER 15

The premiere of "Holy Scratchers," a documentary film about the plight of Palestinian DJs, screened at the Los Angeles International Film Festival to high praise. Warren and Sharon Lopez walked onstage with Kale and his little sister Quinoa to a standing ovation. Photographers flashed bulbs and called out questions. Some of the movie's cast stood onstage as well, including an NFL-sized hype man named Shark Tooth X, who looked and sounded suspiciously like the terrorist Sheik, but no one was the wiser.

In the crowd, the cast of *Natural Dish-aster: Season Five* hooted wildly. Tanya and Brandon, Cowboy and Clora, Nisha and Ghana, Joaquim with two young starlets on his arm, and the rest of the cast.

Also in attendance was Genevieve Jennings, newly installed Senior Vice President of Original Programming at the Network, along with her ingénue, *Jihad Kitchen* star Salid, looking as handsome and tiny as ever.

SALID & JENNINGS (DUAL INTERVIEW)

JENNINGS (INT.): "We are thrilled to be here promoting the launch of the Network's next big hit, *Jihad Kitchen*. But don't let me tell you. Here's the star himself! Tell them how excited you are, Salid."

SALID (INT.): "I have brought great shame upon my family and my people."

JENNINGS (INT.): "Ha, Ha! Oh, Salid, you little kidder! Can you believe this guy? One of the reasons I signed him— he's got that edgy sense of humor I think will resonate with our younger viewership. You know what they say: 'Chefs are the new stand-up comics!'"

SALID (INT.): "No one says that."

JENNINGS (INT.): "The important thing is the launch— we are delighted at what is sure to be an enduring hit for the Network. The food is delicious and exotic, and Salid is a true culinary genius. His dishes should be framed and put in the Louvre."

SALID (INT.): "Then why do you insist I blow them up?"

JENNINGS (INT.): "Salid…"

SALID (INT.): "If you signed me for my culinary artistry, why then ask me to destroy the dishes on camera? It's sacrilege."

JENNINGS (INT.) (smiles to camera): "Ha, oh, there he goes again! A regular Louis CK. Um, Matt, can we just stop shooting for one quick sec? Thanks… (whispering) Salid, we discussed this over and over. American viewers need a hook."

SALID (INT.): "Strapping suicide bombs to food?"

JENNINGS (INT.): "Research paints a clear picture. They want a jihadist they can trust. Someone relatable. Someone they wouldn't mind inviting over for Thanksgiving dinner."

SALID (INT.): "I'm not a jihadist. How many times must I…"

JENNINGS (INT.): "Let's just shelve this, 'kay? This for the Upfronts…"

PRODUCER (off camera): "Do you guys need a minute? Crew wants to break for meal anyway."

JENNINGS (INT.): "No need! We are ready, Freddy. Ha! You know talent, right? Even with their own kitchen [she nudges Salid], all those costly ingredients they asked for to develop original recipes [nudges Salid], and visa applications pending for their entire family [double nudges Salid], they can still get testy. Blue M&M's and all that, right? Heh-heh. Now smile big, Salid. This is for the poster... And say 'jihad'!

SALID (INT.) (forces smile): "Jihad."

Yes, all was well in the land of reality TV. In a media landscape where streaming services were ruling the awards season, The Network was still up a strong six percent in the demos, and that's what counts for Ad Sales. *Natural Dish-aster* was a big part of that success. As Co-EP, there was even a nice little tribute to Sara Sinek out in the theatre lobby. "An industry treasure, gone far too soon," read the text under her photo.

WARREN & SHARON LOPEZ (DUAL INTERVIEW)

WARREN LOPEZ (INT.): "In the end, what did we really know about Sara Sinek? Turns out not as much as we thought. She was former U.S. military, possibly an Israeli spy. Secretly a jihadist herself? That seems far-fetched. Did she attempt to betray the Network, or to save its butt? Also, hard to tell. Best to limit her legacy to what we know. Sara was a solid industry professional, and a hell of a showrunner. She was a loving sister to her brother, Nathan, and supportive daughter to a mother afflicted with a serious gambling addiction. She cared deeply about family, and what's more admirable than that?"

SHARON LOPEZ (INT.) (adoringly): "Oh, Warren. That was really well said."

WARREN (INT.): "Better be—you wrote it..." [They kiss. Warren peeks over her shoulder at his cell phone.]

SHARON (INT.): "Wait, did you just... did you just check your Doucheberry behind my back?"

WARREN (INT.): "It was a text. Could have been the nanny."

SHARON (INT.): "I just listened to you blather on endlessly about family commitment and you can't even kiss your wife without checking your… Wow, you *are* your father's son!"

WARREN (INT.): "Always bringing up my father… She's always bringing up my father! Glad it's finally on tape."

SHARON (INT.): "Try getting laid again this millennium, bub."

WARREN (INT.): "What'd I do?"

Outside on the red carpet, the cast's branded food trucks served deliciousness to hungry patrons dressed in semi-formal attire. Cowboy and Clora leaned out the window of their "culinary chuck wagon," *The Spur,* to serve triple-speed, pickle-brined rib eye *au-poivre* with smoky mayo, alongside Clora's "soul food bahn mi" sandwich with dill pickle emulsion, tiger shrimp, and veal meatballs.

CLORA & COWBOY (DUAL INTERVIEW):

COWBOY (INT.): "Me and Clora are happy as a couple of summer peaches, ain't we, baby doll?"

CLORA (INT.): "Our wedding had this awesome jug band playing spoons and washboards in a rustic barn overlooking a ranch. My sisters did all the flowers, in red of course. And even though his family is all like Trump-supporting cowboys, we had them dressed in traditional Vietnamese robes, chewing areca nuts with my mom and dad. We even served them roasted suckling pig!"

COWBOY (INT.): "Picture my clan in silk robes with all these dragons, and then ten-gallon hats, right? Anything for my baby doll…"

CLORA (INT.): "Awww…"

Etienne and Chrissy's truck, *Foutre Le Pain,* was a main attraction on the carpet. They served their now-famous bird-shaped pastry, *La Junk,* but also an expanded menu of smoked gouda and rachbier soup and minted saké sea shooters. The crowd slurped it up.

With the success of her Instagram feed during the *Natural Dish-aster* shoot, Tanya had leaned hard into her Jewish roots. Her truck, *The Fresser*, served latka with gravlax, coffee-braised brisket, and tehina lentils. Brandon, who was in the process of converting to Judaism at Tanya's behest and wore both kippah and tallit, added molecular gastronomy to the offerings, serving his Hummus Pitry out of emu eggshells that smoked with dry ice.

TANYA & BRANDON (DUAL INTERVIEW):

TANYA (INT.): "I was going to serve tiger shrimp with the lentils, but Brandon here is like… Actually go ahead, honey, you said it."

BRANDON (INT.): "I said, That's *trayf!*'" [Hebrew for "not kosher."]

TANYA (INT.) (gleaming): "Ha! Isn't he just everything?!"

BRANDON (INT.): "Does that mean I finally get to meet your parents?"

TANYA (INT.): "Totally!"

BRANDON (INT.): "You've said that before…"

TANYA (INT.): "Patience, baby. In due time…"

BRANDON (INT.): "In due time… You know what? [demic'ing] I'm outta here. And to think I was about to get circumcised for you! What a joke…"

TANYA (INT.): "Brandon, wait! Come back!"

BRANDON (INT.) (off camera): "What, Tanya? Just… what?"

TANYA (INT.): "Can you let me announce our breakup on Instagram first?"

BRANDON (INT.) (off camera): *bleeped.

TANYA (INT.) (shrugs to camera): "What's with him?"

Ghana and Nisha, who now lived together with Ghana's kids, had teamed up to create their own food truck, *The Carbo-Load*, which served a variety of toast dressed with everything from foie gras, salted cantaloupe, and curried vindaloo.

NISHA (INT.): "I said to Ghana, 'You know what's ridiculous? The war against bread.' I was like, 'Toast. That's my jam.'"

GHANA (INT.): "Ha, you said *jam*."

NISHA (INT.) (to camera): "See, we serve a variety of..."

GHANA (INT.): "I think they got it, Bae."

NISHA (INT.): "Awww, you called me Bae! Kiss me on TV. I want everyone to see I'm your main bae."

GHANA (INT.) (kisses her): "You'll always be my main bae."

Joaquim watched the expanding crowd surrounding Ghana and Nisha's truck and shook his head in disgust. "I loathe food gimmicks," he said.

"Says the dude who coined the term '*piecaken*,'" retorted Cowboy. They both flipped each other the bird.

JOAQUIM (INT.): "Seriously, though, who serves toast with duckfat mousseline and squid ink on butcher paper?"

CHRISSY (INT.): "It was nice to see the crew back together again. And so strong of them not to act jealous when my vegan artisanal ice pops cart got mobbed."

The lines were long and the chefs worked tirelessly. But just as the last of the patrons were served, a familiar voice boomed out over a megaphone: "A great chef must always be ready to improvise," CJ Bazemore said. "So now, consistent with the theme of Holy Scratchers, you must create a completely new appetizer from *scratch*, and like the DJs, use only your hands to create it. That's right, all cooking utensils will be removed completely from your trucks."

Bazemore arched an eyebrow and a team of producers mounted the cast's trucks and began to remove their cooking implements. A collective groan came over the cast of *Natural Dish-aster: Season Five*.

"Not my barbeque tweezers!" hollered Cowboy.

"My immersion circulator!" complained Etienne.

"Hands off my steampunk pepper mill, ya bastards!" yelled

Joaquim.

"That's right," Bazemore continued. "No knives, forks, tongs, microprane graters, whiskers, or spatulas. Like the DJs of Palestine, you must use only your hands to cook. And you better hurry, because you will only have ten minutes to complete your dishes."

CJ Bazemore stepped aside to share the stage with the newest Network star. Jennings nudged the sheepish Salid forward.

"Now, to tell you what's at stake in this competition, the star of *Jihad Kitchen* … Salid!" Bazemore kissed Salid on both cheeks and handed him the megaphone.

"Hello," Salid muttered, eyes downcast. "The winner of this challenge will host their own virtual reality web-series for the Network, and also win five thousand dollars from Oakley's Beans. Oakley's Beans, the best beans in the business."

JOAQUIM (INT.): "Fuck the five grand! I want that VR web series! You guys realize cable TV is dead, right? You think a kid cares if something's on the Network? It's all apps now. And I'm going to be the face of that shit."

"Hands where I can see 'em, Ghana," complained LizZ. "Bazemore didn't say 'go' yet!"

"Focus on your own-self, LizZ. I got this."

"Only thing you got is a view of my tailpipe as I drive right past your massive haul."

"Did you just call me fat?" said Ghana. "Did she just call me fat? Ms. Jennings, I want to talk to HR immediately."

"I was talking about your truck," said LizZ.

"Tell it to my lawyer."

"Oh, it's on now, boy!" said Cowboy with a "yee-haw."

And the chaos continued…

Many hundreds of miles away in a computer lab at The Newberry Academy, just outside of Reno, Nevada, Nathan Sinek signed on for unsupervised game time. A pretty girl his age walked by and waved tentatively, and Nathan waved back. He looked around to see if anyone else was watching and then signed on to Minecraft: Survival Mode. He scanned his list of potential online combatants. "Sara" was still unlit in gray. Nathan sighed.

Since his mom had checked into that expensive rehab, there was almost no one left in his family to chat with. A popup came onto the screen: "A New Minecraft User has entered. Do you want to interact with *Chasing_Pavement?*" Nathan's face spread into a smile. He pressed "yes."

"Ruti?" he typed.

"Call me Adele," came the reply.

"Ready to have your butt kicked again?" he wrote.

"Bring it," wrote Ruti.

In a medical clinic in a small Israeli village on the northern border of Gaza, Ruti signed off of Minecraft: Survival Mode and shut down her computer. She pulled off her nursing scrubs, put on some sweats, and walked out into the waiting room, where anxious mothers soothed babies with sore throats and ear infections. A plaque next to a small play area cited the generous financial contribution of a group known only as "With The Angels."

Ruti was almost at the exit when she noticed a mother at check-in holding a screaming baby whose arm was stuck in a long white vase.

"Half an hour?!" the mother cried. "But my baby is in pain!"

"Then pull her arm out of the vase," said the clerk at the counter.

"But it will hurt her!" said the mother, and the baby screamed even louder.

"I got this," Ruti cut in. She pulled out her medical gloves.

"Oh thank you," the woman said. "Are you a doctor?"

"A nurse," said Ruti. "Do me a favor, sign in and I'll take you to the doctor right now. I can hold her while you fill it out."

"Yes, of course," the woman said.

The woman handed Ruti the screaming baby and leaned over to fill out the paperwork. She had not yet touched pen to paper when the baby's screaming ceased. She looked up to see Ruti holding the vase in one hand and the baby in the other. The baby cooed.

"No charge," Ruti said, handing the baby back to her mother.

"But how?" the woman said.

"Force," Ruti said. "Sometimes it works best." Then she headed out the door.

Tough Israeli chick.

ACKNOWLEDGEMENTS

Deeply grateful to Nancy Foley, Emily Schultz, Brian Joseph Davis, David Bell, and Tim Hedberg for suffering through early drafts of this book and being so incredibly helpful in your feedback. Thank you, brave saints!

Want to thank Kevin Lee, who brought me into the TV business and has always been a great friend and mentor.

And to my pal Brian Lando, who guided me onto the network side, affording me the opportunity to work with so many talented chefs, producers, and food personalities.

To the good folks at Bancroft Press and Publisher Bruce Bortz for believing in this book, and for being a dream to work with at every step of the process.

Finally: to my favorite reader Evan Oliver, to my parents Analee Stein and Joe Oliver, to Bonita Blazer, and to my brother Dave whose support and encouragement is always gold.

And of course to my darling wife Liz, who goads me to write, sometimes by cooking up *shakshuka* with a side of homemade, world-altering hummus. Love you.

ABOUT THE AUTHOR

Jeff Oliver is Vice President of Current Production at Bravo TV. He is a former Food Network producer and executive with credits that include "Big Brother," "Last Comic Standing," and "The Simple Life." At Food Network, Jeff oversaw some of the network's most successful shows, including "Cupcake Wars,""Worst Cooks In America," "Food Network Star," and "Chef Wanted

Author Photo by Stuart Tyson stuarttysonphoto.com

With Anne Burrell." He also developed the long-running series "Cutthroat Kitchen," as well as Cooking Channel's "The Freshman Class" and "The Culinary Adventures Of Baron Ambrosia."

Prior to being at Food Network, Jeff was a freelance Supervising Producer in Los Angeles working with production companies that included Magical Elves, Bunim/Murray Productions, Ryan Seacrest Productions, and World of Wonder. A graduate of McGill University, Jeff has an MFA in Fiction from Brooklyn College (CUNY), and his debut novel, "Failure to Thrive," was published by DC Books.

Jeff's wife, Liz Blazer, is an award-winning filmmaker, art director, visual artist, designer, animator, and educator. She also happens to have co-designed the "Two Plate" book cover.

The two live together in suburban New York City with their son.